His brother's wife.

Emily's words rang in Dillon's head: *You don't even like me.*

Dillon snorted.

He supposed he shouldn't be surprised she believed that. By his actions these past seven years—avoiding her whenever he could, keeping his distance during family gatherings—he had made it appear that way.

How would Emily react, Dillon wondered, if she knew the truth? That all these years, since before his brother had swept her off her feet and married her, he had been in love with her.

And that the baby she now carried was not her late husband's, as she believed.

It was his….

Dear Reader,

This May, we celebrate Mother's Day and a fabulous month of uplifting romances. I'm delighted to introduce RITA® Award finalist Carol Stephenson, who debuts with her heartwarming reunion romance, *Nora's Pride*. Carol writes, "*Nora's Pride* is very meaningful to me, as my mother, my staunchest fan and supporter, passed away in May 2000. I'm sure she's smiling down at me from heaven. She passionately believed this would be my first sale." A must-read for your list!

The Princess and the Duke, by Allison Leigh, is the second book in the CROWN AND GLORY series. Here, a princess and a duke share a kiss, but can their love withstand the truth about a royal assassination? We have another heart-thumper from the incomparable Marie Ferrarella with *Lily and the Lawman*, a darling city-girl-meets-small-town-boy romance.

In *A Baby for Emily*, Ginna Gray delivers an emotionally charged love story in which a brooding hero lays claim to a penniless widow who, unbeknownst to her, is carrying *their* child.... Sharon De Vita pulls on the heartstrings with *A Family To Come Home To*, in which a rugged rancher searches for his family and finds true love! You also won't want to miss Patricia McLinn's *The Runaway Bride*, a humorous tale of a sexy cowboy who rescues a distressed bride.

I hope you enjoy these exciting books from Silhouette Special Edition—the place for love, life and family. Come back for more winning reading next month!

Sincerely,

Karen Taylor Richman
Senior Editor

Ginna Gray

A BABY FOR EMILY

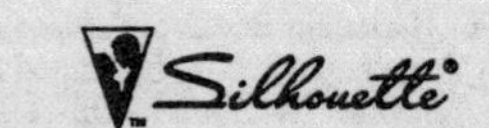

SPECIAL EDITION™

Published by Silhouette Books
America's Publisher of Contemporary Romance

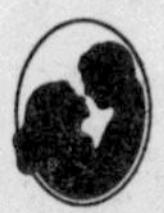

SILHOUETTE BOOKS

ISBN 0-373-24466-5

A BABY FOR EMILY

This edition published by arrangement with Harlequin Books S.A.

Visit Silhouette at www.eHarlequin.com

Printed in U.S.A.

Books by Ginna Gray

Silhouette Special Edition

Golden Illusion #171
The Heart's Yearning #265
Sweet Promise #320
Cristen's Choice #373
**Fools Rush In* #416
**Where Angels Fear* #468
If There Be Love #528
**Once in a Lifetime* #661
**A Good Man Walks In* #722
**Building Dreams* #792
**Forever* #854
**Always* #891
The Bride Price #973
Alissa's Miracle #1117
**Meant for Each Other* #1221
†*A Man Apart* #1330
†*In Search of Dreams* #1340
†*The Ties That Bind* #1395
A Baby for Emily #1466

Silhouette Romance

The Gentling #285
The Perfect Match #311
Heart of the Hurricane #338
Images #352
First Love, Last Love #374
The Courtship of Dani #417
Sting of the Scorpion #826

Silhouette Books

Silhouette Christmas Stories 1987
"Season of Miracles"

Wanted: Mother 1996
"Soul Mates"

*The Blaines and the McCalls of Crockett, Texas
†A Family Bond

GINNA GRAY

A native Texan, Ginna Gray lived in Houston all her life until 1993, when she and her husband, Brad, built their "dream home" and moved to the mountains of Colorado. Coming from a large Irish/American family, in which spinning colorful yarns was commonplace, made writing a natural career choice for Ginna. "I grew up hearing so many fascinating tales, I was eleven or twelve before I realized that not everyone made up stories," Ginna says. She sold her first novel in 1983 and has been working as a full-time writer ever since. She has also given many lectures and writing workshops and judged in writing contests. The mother of two grown daughters, Ginna also enjoys other creative activities, such as oil painting, sewing, sketching, knitting and needlepoint.

NEW MEXICO
OKLAHOMA
ARKANSAS
Fort Worth
Dallas
LOUISIANA
TEXAS
Houston
San Antonio
N
MEXICO
Gulf of Mexico

Chapter One

She's hanging on by a thread.

Dillon Maguire ground his teeth. He stood alone in the bay window alcove, a little apart from the others, his intense gaze fixed on his sister-in-law.

Sitting on one of the twin living room sofas flanking the fireplace with her hands folded in her lap, Emily Collins Maguire stared into the middle distance at nothing. For the most part she seemed oblivious to the other mourners crowded into her posh, northwest Houston home. Whenever someone approached her, she raised stricken eyes and murmured a few words, even attempted a watery smile, but as soon as the person moved away she withdrew again into her own private hell.

Dammit, it was barbaric to put her through this, Dillon silently raged. And for what? To honor a man who, in dying, had revealed himself to be without honor?

Dillon glanced around at the other people milling through the impressive house. The fierceness of his gaze caused several of those nearby to regard him with alarm and retreat a few paces.

Just look at them, he thought with disgust. Look at them! Swilling wine and devouring the buffet meal. They huddled together in little groups, chatting among themselves, even laughing discreetly, all the while casting sidelong glances at the widow and whispering behind their hands.

Some were neighbors and friends. A few were family, but most of these people had been Keith's colleagues at St. John's General Hospital. Did they see so much death and human agony that they were inured to Emily's pain? To the humiliation she was suffering?

Oh sure, the doctors and nurses and other hospital staff had all been shocked by the unexpected death of one of their own, and no doubt Dr. Keith Wesley Maguire would be missed. However, Dillon suspected that a lot of these people had come to the funeral, and now the wake, not so much to show respect or to grieve, but out of a sick desire to see how the widow was holding up.

And, of course, to rehash and relish this juicy scandal.

Keith himself had often laughed about what a hotbed of gossip St. John's was. And it wasn't every day, after all, that one of the medical community's most esteemed oncologists died in bed with his mistress.

Though the firemen had managed to put out the blaze before it reached Keith and his lover, the pair had died in their sleep of asphyxiation, wrapped in each other's arms, naked. Later it had been revealed that the mortgage on the apartment was in Keith's name.

Dillon's gaze went back to Emily, and his mouth tightened. On the surface she appeared to be hanging in there, but she was pale as bleached flour. And so tense and fragile she looked as though she might shatter into a million pieces at any moment. Like brittle glass.

No small wonder.

That Emily had received the most joyous news of her life only hours earlier had made Keith's death doubly devastating. In the space of just a few hours she had gone from euphoria to the depths of despair.

Dillon could not even imagine how she must feel. His own grief was a crushing, hollow ache in his chest, as though someone had cut out his heart with a dull knife. He didn't know which was worse—the pain of losing his brother, or the anger that threatened to consume him.

A tiny muscle rippled in Dillon's cheek as his jaw clenched tighter. Damn you, Keith. *Damn* you! How could you do this to her?

His heart pounded against his ribs, but it was only when the rattle of china drew his gaze downward that he realized he was shaking with fury. He stared at the cup, dancing in its saucer, the quivering, shiny surface of the coffee that he hadn't touched, surprised that he still held it.

''You're Keith's brother, aren't you?''

Dillon looked up from placing the cup on the grand piano and found himself facing a slender man in his late thirties. His face was vaguely familiar. An instant later Dillon recognized him as one of the partners in the medical group where Keith had practiced.

The man stuck out his hand. ''I'm Dr. Garrett Conn, one of Keith's partners. We met once, several years ago, but you probably don't remember me. I just wanted to tell you how sorry I am for your loss.''

Shaking the doctor's hand, Dillon murmured the expected thanks, but that was all. The man had kind eyes and there was compassion in his voice and expression, but Dillon remained wary. If Dr. Conn was hoping to get the sordid details from him he was barking up the wrong tree.

''Your brother was an excellent physician. Our practice won't be the same without him. He'll be sorely missed.'' Dr. Conn folded his mouth into a thin line and shook his head. ''Such a waste.''

He paused, as though waiting for a response, but Dillon merely fixed him with a level stare. After a moment the doctor went on. ''I suppose, being as you're Keith's older brother, you'll be looking after Emily now?''

Dillon's eyes narrowed. ''Why do you ask?''

A wry smile twisted the other man's mouth. ''Keith always said you were an intimidating bastard. Relax. I'm not trying to pump you for information, if that's what you think. Your brother's affairs don't interest me. I leave that sort of tittle-tattle to others,'' he said with a nod toward a group of people on the other side of the room. ''I approached you because Emily is my patient, and I'm worried about her.''

The statement had no effect on Dillon's stern expression. ''Emily's doctor is Frank Young,'' he challenged. He knew that because the whole family went to Dr. Young.

"Yes, Frank is the G.P. in our practice. My specialty is gynecology and obstetrics."

Dillon tensed. He shot a sharp glance at Emily, then swung back to Dr. Conn. "Is there a problem with the baby?"

The doctor's eyes widened. "You know about that?"

"Yes. Keith told me."

"I see. Actually, that's a relief. I wasn't sure that he and Emily had shared the news with anyone. Now at least I don't have to worry about betraying doctor-patient confidentiality."

"You didn't answer my question. Is there a problem?"

"It's too soon to tell. The in vitro was performed only last week and the pregnancy confirmed three days ago—just hours before Keith died in that fire. But I have to tell you, the shock of his death, particularly given the circumstances, has put an enormous strain on Emily, and that's never good."

"Are you saying she could lose the baby?"

"After emotional trauma like that it's certainly possible. I talked to her earlier, and she says she's okay, but I'm concerned. She's strung tighter than a fiddle string and too pale by far. Has she mentioned having any problems?"

"No. At least, not to me." But then, he'd be the last person Emily would turn to for help, especially with something as personal as that. She avoided him whenever she could. "Actually, I don't think she's told anyone she's pregnant. I doubt she even knows that Keith told me."

Keith had called him from his car phone that night. God, had it been only seventy-two hours ago? His brother had said that he was on the way to the hospital to see a patient, but in reality he'd been heading to meet up with his mistress.

Typical, Dillon thought with disgust. Instead of sharing the joy of impending parenthood with his wife, his faithless brother had chosen to celebrate by tearing up the sheets with his latest girlfriend.

"Mmm." Dr. Conn studied Emily from across the room. "It would be a good idea if someone stayed with her, at least for the next few days until she gets over the initial shock."

"Don't worry. I'll see to it."

"Good, good. Tell her if she experiences so much as a twinge to call me, day or night." He gave Dillon a sympathetic smile. "Look, I just want you to know that despite his faults, I truly liked your brother. He was a good doctor and a good friend. I know this is a terrible time for you and your family. If there's anything I can do to help—anything at all—just let me know."

"If you really mean that, how about nudging your friends toward the door," Dillon said, nodding toward the clutch of people on the other side of the room. "Emily's had a rough couple of days. She needs to rest." And she needs a chance to lick her wounds in private, he added silently.

Dr. Conn chuckled. "I'll see what I can do."

When the doctor walked away Dillon's gaze zeroed in on Emily again, a new worry niggling at him. Why *hadn't* she told anyone about the baby? He'd been waiting for her to mention her condition ever since the night of Keith's death, but she hadn't said a word.

He studied her delicate profile, her blank expression. What are you feeling? he wondered. Anger? Hurt? Humiliation? Grief?

Hell, she had to be feeling all those things and more, he decided. And who could blame her? Well...who besides Adele, at any rate? His mother always blamed others for Keith's mistakes and shortcomings.

But what about the new life inside her? How did Emily feel about the baby now? She had wanted a child so badly, and had gone to extreme lengths to conceive. However, now Keith was gone and she'd had her blinders ripped off in the cruelest way possible. Now that she'd learned just what a louse of a husband he'd truly been, did she regret the pregnancy?

Oh, hell, did she want to end it?

Worse, if she had the baby would she resent him or her and reject the child?

As his mother rejected him?

Reluctantly, Dillon's gaze switched to his mother. Adele Maguire and Dillon's sister Charlotte, and her husband, Roger Boyd, sat on the sofa opposite the one Emily occupied. Clinging to her daughter for support, Adele wailed and wept bitterly and ignored Emily.

Dillon's mouth curled. As far as Adele was concerned, no one, not even Keith's widow, could possibly be experiencing the pain and loss that she felt over his death.

The prospect of a grandchild—particularly Keith's child—might mitigate Adele's grief somewhat, Dillon mused. More importantly, it might even make her more accepting of the daughter-in-law she had merely tolerated for the past seven years. Emily had to know that. Still, she kept silent. Why?

Dillon was still pondering that when Dr. Conn and the other partners and their wives approached Emily and his family to offer final condolences and bid them goodbye. Noting with relief that others were beginning to collect their coats as well, Dillon went to see them out.

For what seemed like hours, he stood in the foyer, shaking hands and accepting condolences and perfunctory offers of help. By the time he closed the door behind the last person his patience was almost at an end.

"Well, that's it," he announced, returning to the living room. "All the wagging tongues have finally left."

His sister's two children, Leslie and Roy, had retreated to the den at the back of the house to watch television. In the dining room Ila Mae, Emily's housekeeper, had already started putting away the leftover food and gathering up the stray dishes scattered around.

Adele dabbed at her eyes with a tissue and shot him an annoyed look. "Must you always be so crass?"

Dillon shrugged. "Ignoring the truth doesn't change it. I've never heard so much malicious whispering in one place before. But I suppose you have to expect that when someone gets caught practically in the act."

Emily made a small, distressed sound and turned her face away, and Dillon immediately winced.

"Sorry, Emily," he murmured.

He could have kicked himself. Dammit, man, what

were you thinking? Maybe his mother was right. Maybe he was a thoughtless clod.

Adele sniffed and dabbed her eyes again. "I don't know why everyone is being so unkind and judgmental. It should be obvious that if my son turned to another woman then he wasn't getting the affection and emotional support he needed at home."

"Dammit to hell!" Dillon roared.

Charlotte closed her eyes and groaned.

"Well, I'm sorry, but it's the truth," Adele insisted with an indignant lift of her chin.

"The hell it is!" Towering over his mother, Dillon jabbed the air with his forefinger, just inches from her nose. "Don't you *dare* try to blame this on Emily."

"No, Dillon, please," Emily murmured. "It...it doesn't matter. Really."

"It matters," he insisted, never taking his furious gaze off of Adele. "All of his life, no matter what underhanded thing Keith did, no matter what mistakes he made, no matter who he hurt, you made excuses for him. It was always someone else's fault, never your precious Keith's. Well, if you think I'm going to let you get away with it this time, think again."

"How dare you sa—!"

"Oh, I dare. Your precious son cheated on his wife because he was spoiled rotten, thanks to your coddling. He grew up thinking the world revolved around him and that he should have whatever he wanted when he wanted it, regardless of who he hurt. Face it, professionally, he may have been a respected doctor, but on a personal level he was selfish, self-centered and incapable of fidelity."

"How can you be so cruel?" Adele wailed. "That

you, of all people, would talk about Keith that way. He was your *brother!*''

''And I loved him. But, dammit, I wasn't blind to his faults.''

He took off his suit coat, dropped it onto a chair, then stripped off his tie and tossed it on top. By the time he had unfastened the top three buttons on his shirt Adele looked as though she'd swallowed a lemon. Paying her no mind, he exhaled a long sigh and muttered a heartfelt, ''Thank God. For the past eight hours that thing has felt like a noose around my neck.''

''You'd be accustomed to wearing proper attire if you did so more often,'' his mother said with a disdainful sniff.

''I hate wearing suits and ties.''

Just as he hated being cooped up in a fancy office. Over the years, as his company had grown and prospered, he'd had to endure both more and more—especially when he met with bankers or attorneys or clients. Thankfully, he was still able to spend much of his time on the construction sites in a hard hat and work clothes.

Adele dabbed at her eyes again. ''I don't know why I try. You'll never be anything but a common workman.''

Though she meant it as an insult, Dillon wasn't offended. In his opinion there was nothing demeaning about good, honest labor. He liked working with his hands as well as his mind, and he was proud of what he'd accomplished.

Besides, he wondered how many ''common workmen'' his mother knew who owned a multimillion-dollar construction company? One they'd built from the ground up on their own?

He kept quiet, however. Defending himself to her was pointless. No matter what he said or did, she would find fault.

Adele loved Charlotte well enough, but Keith had always been her favorite, her "golden boy" as she was fond of calling him. In her eyes, Keith could do no wrong...and Dillon could do no right. It was a fact of life that he had accepted long ago.

Emily barely registered the exchange between Dillon and Adele. Her anger and hurt had turned to a deep, dark feeling that hung around her shoulders like a lead cape, weighing her down so much she could barely function. She longed to climb into bed and curl up into a ball of misery beneath the covers and shut out the world. The last thing she wanted right now was to be around people, especially Keith's family.

She started when Dillon sank down on the sofa next to her. He'd left the space of a cushion between them, but just having him that close made her feel crowded. Uneasy.

Dillon always had that effect on her. He towered a foot over her puny five feet four inches, but it was more than that. There were those massive shoulders and bulging biceps, those big, callused hands. His brawny chest tapered down to a washboard abdomen and narrow hips that any male model would envy. Dillon was such a physical man and so overwhelmingly masculine he almost gave off an aura. Whenever she was around him she felt it hitting her in waves.

Stretching his long legs out in front of him, he heaved a long sigh. "Thank heaven that's over."

Emily gripped her hands together tighter and briefly closed her eyes, perilously close to tears. Dear Lord, he can't be half as thankful as I am, she thought. Now if they would all just go home, as well, and leave her alone.

Word of Keith's infidelity and the sordid details of his death had spread like wildfire. She had been aware of the pitying looks and whispered comments that had swirled around her all day. It had taken every ounce of pride and strength that she possessed just to get through the funeral and the wake with her head held high, but the strain had taken its toll. She felt shaky and fragile, as though every nerve ending in her body was frayed and threatening to give way.

If she was going to fall apart, she wanted to do so in private, not in front of Keith's family. Especially not in front of Dillon.

From the beginning he had not liked her, nor had he approved of her marrying Keith. He was always so somber and remote, so in control. She was fairly certain he would disapprove of even the hint of hysteria on her part. Besides, she had no intention of allowing him to see her that vulnerable.

"There was a nice turnout for the service," Charlotte offered lamely to fill the uncomfortable silence that had stretched out.

Adele sniffed. "Of course. Why wouldn't there be? Everyone loved Keith. He was a wonderful man and a prominent, respected physician. He was also handsome, bright and utterly charming.

"And the most wonderful son any mother could ask for," she added in a quavery voice as fresh tears welled in her eyes. With a choked sob, she buried her face in her hands again and gave in to another storm of weeping.

He was also a womanizing cheat, Emily added silently, but she kept the thought to herself. There was no point in angering Adele. In her mother-in-law's eyes, her younger son had been perfect, and nothing anyone could say would convince her otherwise.

Dillon's mouth twisted as he stared pityingly at his mother, but he said nothing.

Patting Adele's heaving shoulders, Charlotte rocked her back and forth and murmured words of comfort.

"Excuse me, Miz Maguire." Ila Mae appeared in the arched doorway leading into the foyer, wiping her hands on her apron. "I'm finished. The food is stored away, kitchen is cleaned and the dishes are washing in the machine. Is there anything else you'd like me to do before I leave?"

"No. Thank you, Ila Mae."

"I hate to leave you here in this big house all alone. You sure you don't want me to stay the night? My mister would understand."

"No, really. That won't be necessary. I'll be fine."

When Ila Mae had gone Charlotte looked at Dillon again over the top of their mother's head. "I think Roger and I had better take Mother home now, too. I'll give her a sedative and put her to bed."

"Good idea," Dillon agreed.

"I'll go round up the kids," Roger volunteered and headed for the den.

Emily barely resisted the urge to sigh with relief. Thank heavens.

"Yes. Yes, take me home," Adele cried. "There's nothing left for me here. My wonderful son is gone."

Emily pressed her lips together. She knew that Adele's grief was genuine, but her mother-in-law's constant lauding of Keith was like pouring salt into an open wound. Emily just wanted them all to go.

Finally everyone was bundled into their winter coats and gloves, but Adele's mouth began to quiver piteously again as they prepared to leave. She cast a tragic look around the foyer as though she expected never to return, and whimpered, "I still can't believe he's gone. That I'll never see my son again."

She turned an accusing look on Dillon. "If I had to lose a son it should have been you. Not my Keith."

"Mother!"

"Adele!" Charlotte and Emily gasped in unison.

"Oh, Mother, how could you? That's a horrible thing to say."

Adele looked away, her mouth pinched so tight the tiny creases around her lips radiated like a starburst. "I'm sorry, but I can't help it. That's how I feel."

Emily was so shocked that for the first time in three days she forgot about her own pain. She stared at her mother-in-law and wondered how she could utter such a heartless statement, no matter how grief-stricken. Especially to one of her own children.

"She didn't mean it, Dillon," Charlotte insisted, laying her hand on her brother's arm. "She's just upset, that's all."

"Don't worry about it, sis." He shrugged off the cruel comment as though it meant no more to him than an offhand remark from a stranger.

Dillon bid Roger good-night, kissed and hugged Charlotte and the kids, and, to Emily's surprise, dutifully kissed Adele's cheek. She turned her head away at the last instant, barely allowing his lips to graze her skin, and even though it was Dillon, Emily felt terrible for him.

When at last they were gone she closed the door and turned to him with a sympathetic look. "Charlotte is right, you know. She really didn't mean it."

"She meant it."

"Oh, no. You mustn't think that. That was just grief talking. Adele loves you."

Dillon gave her an under-the-brow look. "C'mon, Emily. You've been in this family for seven years. You know better than that."

He turned and headed back into the living room. Emily hurried after him.

"I know that Adele isn't always nice to you—"

"Now there's an understatement."

"And I know that Keith was her favorite," she continued. "I'm not condoning that, mind you. I don't think it's right for a parent to favor one child over another. But just because Adele did that doesn't mean she doesn't love you, too. Mothers love their children, no matter what."

Resuming his seat, Dillon stretched his legs out in front of him, rested his head against the sofa back and looked at her from beneath half-closed eyes. "Yeah, that's what they say. But it doesn't always work out that way. As far back as I can remember she's never been able to stomach the sight of me."

"But—"

"Look, it's okay. That's just the way it is. I accepted it a long time ago."

She opened her mouth to argue more, then shut it again. What was she doing? This was Dillon. The man was self-sufficient, remote and tough as old shoe leather. He didn't need anyone. Apparently not even his own mother. If Adele's hateful comments didn't bother him, why should she be concerned? She had enough pain of her own to deal with. She had neither the will nor the energy to worry about other people's problems.

Wearily, Emily resumed her seat, this time on the sofa across from the one on which Dillon sat. She turned her head and fixed her gaze on the blaze crackling in the fireplace without really seeing it. She felt numb and empty inside, as though her body were just a hollow, aching shell.

How could she have been so blind? Seven years. For seven years she had believed that she had the perfect life—a storybook marriage to a handsome, charming doctor who adored her, a lovely home, an active social life, friends, financial security—all the things she'd dreamed of during her lonely childhood. Now she knew that it had all been an illusion.

Unconsciously, her hand splayed over her flat belly. The only thing that had been missing from hers and Keith's perfect life had been a baby, and he had even managed to give her that in the end.

Was that the problem? Had she been so focused on getting pregnant these past few years that she had lost sight of her husband's needs and desires? Had she neglected him? Had he been unhappy with her?

No. No, she didn't believe that. She and Keith had gotten along beautifully. In seven years they'd rarely had a cross word, for heaven's sake. And Keith had wanted this baby as much as she had. Like her, he had been jubilant when Dr. Conn had telephoned them with the news on Monday afternoon.

So why had he turned to another woman? When had it started?

"Are you all right?"

Emily jumped and her head whipped around. She experienced a little shock when her gaze met Dillon's. She had forgotten he was there.

"I...yes, I'm all right."

"Maybe you ought to turn in. You've had a rough couple of days, and tomorrow isn't going to be a piece of cake either."

"Tomorrow?"

"You meet with your attorney to settle the estate and see where you stand financially. Remember?"

"Oh, yes. That. I'd forgotten."

Emily eyed Dillon's relaxed posture. She had expected him to leave with the others, or at least soon after. Instead he looked as though he had settled in for a long stay.

"You're probably right."

She climbed to her feet, but when Dillon failed to do the same she paused. "Uh, thank you for your help, with the funeral arrangements and all. I really appreciate everything you've done these past couple of days." She began edging toward the door, hoping he'd take the hint. Dillon just continued to watch her from beneath those hooded eyes.

"No thanks necessary."

"Yes, well...thanks anyway."

She edged another few inches closer to the door, but still he didn't move. Emily shifted from one foot to the other and clasped and unclasped her hands. Finally she decided that the best way to deal with Dillon was head-on.

"Uh, I don't mean to be rude, but as you said, I probably ought to try to get some sleep."

"Good idea."

Relief poured through her. With a nod, she turned and started for the foyer again, but his next words brought her up short.

"If you need anything, I'll be in the guest room across the hall from you."

She whirled around. "What?"

"You shouldn't be alone right now. So I'll be staying here for a few days. I put my bag in the guest room earlier."

"No, really, that's not necessary. If I'd wanted company I would've let Ila Mae spend the night. I really do prefer to be alone."

"That may be, but I'm staying."

Emily's nerves began to jump. As her anxiety grew she forgot all about caution. "Look, Dillon, you don't understand. I don't want you here. In case it hasn't occurred to you, at the moment I'm not feeling all that well-disposed toward any male with the name Maguire."

Unfolding himself from his slouched position, he slowly rose to his feet. He towered over her, his face carved in granite. "I'm not Keith, Emily," he said in a voice that cut like honed steel.

Belatedly, she realized that butting heads with Dillon perhaps wasn't the wisest course of action. He was the strong, silent type, but when aroused he had a formidable temper.

In the best of times he intimidated her, and at the moment she was feeling too shaky and beaten down to even attempt to do battle. "Look, I appreciate the offer. Really, I do. But it's unnecessary. I'm fine."

"How about the baby? Is he fine?"

She sucked in a sharp breath and gaped at him, and once again her hand went automatically to her stomach. "How did you—?"

"Keith called me from his car a couple of hours before he died."

Emily's shoulders slumped. She sank down onto the arm of a nearby chair and cupped her hand over her forehead. She should have known. Though they had been as opposite in personality as any two men could be, Keith and Dillon had always been close.

"I see," she said finally. "Well, if it will put your mind at ease, the baby is fine. So you see, there's really no reason for anyone to stay."

"Give it up, Emily. I'm not leaving."

"Why are you doing this?" she snapped in frustration. "You don't even like me."

For an interminable time he simply stared at her. Then he tipped his head toward the stairway in the foyer. "Go to bed, Emily. I'll see you in the morning."

She opened her mouth to argue, then shut it again. With a sigh, she turned and headed for the stairs. She simply didn't have the strength to do battle with him right now.

Dillon remained where he was and watched her go. When she was out of sight he walked over to the drinks cart and poured himself two fingers of Jack Daniels from the crystal decanter. He tossed back half the drink in one gulp, then refilled the glass and wandered over to the window.

He gazed past his reflection into the gloomy night. Sometime since they'd left the cemetery a Texas ''blue norther'' had blown in, turning the weather nasty. Wind whipped the bare trees into a frenzy and sleet clicked against the window panes. Dillon sipped his drink, his face somber, Emily's last words ringing in his head.

You don't even like me.

He snorted. He supposed he shouldn't be surprised that she believed that. In a way, by his actions these past seven years—avoiding her whenever he could, keeping his distance during family gatherings—he had made it appear that way.

Dillon turned away from the window and ambled over to the arched doorway. He leaned a shoulder against the jamb and looked up the stairway in the direction of Emily's bedroom. How would she react, he wondered, if she knew the truth—that all these years, since before his brother had swept her off her feet, he had been in love with her.

And that the baby she carried was not Keith's, as she believed. It was his.

Chapter Two

Emily had barely slept since Keith's death, and that night was no different. Merely knowing that Dillon was across the hall made her uncomfortable, but mostly it was grief and anger that kept sleep at bay.

She lay awake, staring at the ceiling, tormenting herself, imagining her husband with his mistress, laughing with her, kissing her. Making love to her.

Why, Keith? she asked over and over. Why? How could you do this to me when you claimed to love me?

Had she missed something? Had there been signs all along? Subtle indications that her marriage was in trouble? Emily scoured her memory and spent hours soul-searching, but over and over she came up empty.

Keith had seemed perfectly happy with their life together. They never fought, rarely ever exchanged so much as a cross word. They enjoyed each other's company, and their sex life was good.

He had often talked about their future, how, someday he would take a leave from his practice and they would spend a whole summer traveling through Europe, and how when he retired they'd buy a boat and sail around the world.

Emily frowned. Was that it? Could he have been worried that having a child would tie them down?

That didn't seem likely. Keith had been as eager to start a family as she. Well...almost as eager. She had been thinking of little else for the last couple of years. But certainly he'd been overjoyed when Dr. Conn had telephoned them on Monday with the good news.

"So why did you turn to someone else," she whispered to the shadows on the ceiling. Was it her? Something she'd done? Or hadn't done? Wasn't she pretty enough? Smart enough? Interesting enough? Oh, Lord, wasn't she woman enough?

Like bees buzzing in her brain, Emily's thoughts bedeviled her into the wee hours of the morning, until finally exhaustion overtook her. She slept fitfully, and woke a little before eight feeling sluggish and headachy. She was vaguely aware that something was different this morning—something besides Keith's absence—but she was too muzzy-headed to work it out.

She staggered into the adjoining bathroom, downed two Tylenol and stepped into the shower.

Emerging a short while later wrapped in a long, terry-cloth robe, her wet auburn hair combed back from her face, she headed downstairs for a wake-up cup of coffee. The instant she stepped into the hallway and her gaze touched on the guest room, she remembered Dillon.

She stopped and caught her lower lip between her teeth. The door was open, and after a moment she crept across the hall and peeked inside. The bed was made and the room was neat as a pin. There was no sign of Dillon.

Of course, she thought with a sigh of relief as she glanced at the clock on the night stand. This was Friday. He had left for work hours ago.

Tightening the tie belt on her robe, she headed for the stairs.

The aroma of coffee and sausage drifted from the kitchen as she approached the door. Evidently Dillon had made himself breakfast before he left. Emily hoped he'd brewed a full pot of coffee and left some for her.

Pushing open the swinging door, she stepped inside the kitchen and came to a halt. "Dillon. What are you doing here?"

He turned from the stove and cocked an eyebrow at her. "Good morning to you, too." He looked absurdly masculine with a mixing bowl in one hand, a wire whisk in the other and one of Ila Mae's ruffled aprons tied around his lean middle.

He went back to whipping the contents of the bowl with brisk efficiency. "Why are you surprised? I told you last night that I was going to stay here."

"Yes, but...I thought you would be at work by now."

"I'm not going in for a few days."

"Oh, please. You don't have to do that on my account. Haven't you just started an important job? An office complex or something?"

"An indoor shopping mall."

"I see. Well, I wouldn't want to take you away from that."

"No problem. I have an excellent crew. My foreman can handle things for a few days. If something comes up, he has my cell phone number."

He turned back to the stove. "You're just in time for breakfast. I was about to cook pancakes."

Only then did Emily notice that the table was set for two.

Dillon set the bowl and whisk aside, then filled a mug with coffee and plunked it down on the opposite side of the island counter and motioned for her to join him. "The coffee is decaf, so you don't have to worry about hurting the baby. Come on over. You can keep me company."

Keeping company with Dillon was the last thing Emily wanted, but she was still too muzzy-headed to think of an excuse to leave. Giving the belt on her robe another tug, she reluctantly crossed the room and hitched up onto one of the high barstools on the opposite side of the kitchen island from where he was working.

"I, uh…I had no idea you cooked," she said, watching him pour batter onto a hot griddle.

Dillon darted her a look, his blue eyes glinting beneath ebony eyebrows. "There are a lot of things about me that you don't know."

"Yes. I suppose there are," she murmured. Oddly, she felt as though she'd just been chastised, though she couldn't imagine why. Falling silent, she cradled the mug in both hands and sipped her coffee while she watched him deftly flip perfect, golden pancakes.

Despite his success and wealth, she had always thought of Dillon as tough and brawny, slightly rough around the edges, but yesterday at the funeral he had looked astonishingly smart in his custom-made suit. However, this morning, dressed in jeans and an old gray sweatshirt, he looked more like the Dillon she was accustomed to seeing—that is, if you overlooked the apron around his waist. That bit of ruffled material might have made some men look effeminate, but not Dillon. If anything, by stark contrast, it emphasized his compelling maleness.

The sleeves of his sweatshirt were pushed up to his elbows, and Emily's gaze zeroed in on his muscled forearms and broad wrists, sprinkled with short black hair. His big, workman's hands wielded the spatula with amazing grace and dexterity that spoke of long practice.

As always, just being in the same room with Dillon made Emily uneasy. His great size and that staggering masculinity alone were intimidating. Added to that, he was too intense, too remote and brooding.

It was funny how siblings could be so different, she mused, sipping her coffee. In looks, Dillon was a rough-cut version of Keith, bigger, brawnier, more intense, but with the same black hair and clear blue eyes, the same strong facial bone structure. In Keith's case the combination had added up to debonair and handsome, whereas in Dillon's the same features had produced a rugged, harshly masculine face.

In personality, however, Dillon was nothing at all like either his vivacious older sister or his glib, charming younger brother.

He had never been anything but polite to her, yet she'd always sensed that he didn't want her as a sister-in-law.

"There. All done." He came around the end of the

island carrying a platter piled high with pancakes and sausage and put it on the table. "C'mon, let's dig in while it's hot."

"I'm really not much of a breakfast person," Emily began, but he silenced her with a look, and when he held out a chair for her she sighed and slid off the barstool. She just didn't have the energy or the will to fight him.

Dillon settled into the chair across from hers. He picked up the platter and filled first her plate, then his own.

"Oh, no, please. I couldn't possibly eat all this."

"Eat," he commanded, giving her a stern look. "You need to keep your strength up. These past three days you've barely touched your food. That's not good for you or the baby."

She wanted to argue, but of course he was correct. Trust Dillon to hit upon just the right argument. With a sigh, Emily poured syrup over the pancakes and picked up her fork.

Though the food was delicious, she had no appetite, and she had to force herself to take small, nibbling bites. It was as though the grief and depression weighing her down had numbed all her senses. She seemed to be functioning in a haze, oddly disconnected from the world around her—even from her own body. Except for her heart. It was an aching knot in her chest.

They ate in silence for several minutes. Concentrating on finishing her meal and getting out of there, Emily jumped when Dillon spoke.

"Would you answer a question for me?"

Her head came up and she shot him a sharp look. "That depends on the question."

"I know that for years you've been wanting to start

a family, and that you were overjoyed to finally get pregnant, but how do you feel about the baby now?''

''What do you mean?''

''Do you still want it?''

Emily's fork clattered to the plate. She stared at him, stunned. Reflexively, her hand splayed over her flat tummy. ''Of course I do. How could I not? I don't know how you can even ask such a—'' The look on his face stopped her. ''Oh. I see. You mean, now that I know Keith's true colors, do I want his baby?''

''Something like that,'' Dillon admitted, watching her in that intent way he had.

''Just because Keith fathered this child, that doesn't necessarily mean he or she will inherit his character flaws. This will be my child, too.''

''If that's how you feel, then why didn't you tell anyone you were pregnant?''

Emily looked down and fixed her gaze on her fingers, plucking at the napkin in her lap. ''I don't know, exactly,'' she mumbled. ''I just didn't want to.''

Lord, she didn't want to talk about this. She didn't want to talk, period. Or be around anyone. All she wanted was to be left alone. Then she could crawl back into bed and curl up under the covers and give in to the terrible pain and lethargy that threatened to smother her.

''Why not?'' Dillon persisted.

''For one thing, I didn't want to give the wagging tongues anything else to gossip about.'' She kept her gaze lowered, avoiding his, and plucked at the napkin.

''You could've told the family. The news may have mitigated Mother's grief a bit and maybe even gotten her off your back.''

Emily shook her head. ''Actually, if I had a choice,

I'd never tell Adele. You know how she was about Keith. I'm afraid she'll see this baby as a substitute for him and try to take over. Once I tell her, I'm sure I'll have a battle on my hands. I'm just not up to that right now."

Emily raked her spread fingers through her hair. It was almost dry now, and curling around her face and shoulders. "Anyway…I…I wanted to hold on to this one thing, the one bright point in this whole mess. My little secret." She looked at him pleadingly. "Can you understand that?"

"Yeah, I think so. Actually, you're probably doing the smart thing keeping the news from Mother for as long as you can."

"So…you won't tell her?"

One corner of his mouth quirked. "We don't communicate all that often. Trust me, she won't hear it from me."

Emily's shoulders drooped with relief. Despite his less-than-perfect relationship with his mother, she had half expected him to take Adele's side.

"You do realize that you're going to have to tell her eventually, don't you?" he prodded gently. "Pregnancy isn't something you can hide forever."

"I know. But I'd like to put it off for as long as I can." Secretly, she harbored the fantasy that she'd never have to tell her mother-in-law.

Adele had never cared for her. It wasn't personal—at least, Emily didn't think so. Keith's mother simply had not believed any woman was good enough for her precious younger son. Emily didn't expect to hear much from Adele in the future, if she heard from her at all, which suited her just fine.

Listlessly, Emily picked up the fork again. Nibbling a bite of pancake, she let her mind drift. She didn't want to think about that right now. She didn't want to think about anything.

Covertly, Dillon watched the way she picked at her food. She was so withdrawn she was barely conscious of him or anything else. Surely that depth of depression couldn't be endured for long, he thought.

He was trying to think of a way to distract her when the telephone rang, shattering the quiet of the kitchen.

Emily jumped. "Oh, Lord, who can that be? I...I don't want to talk to anyone."

"Take it easy. You don't have to. I'll get it," Dillon said, rising.

Snatching up the receiver of the wall telephone, he growled, "Maguire residence."

"Dillon. I was hoping I'd find you there," his sister said. "I tried calling your place but I got no answer."

"I'm helping Emily with the legal red tape."

"Oh. Well, that's good. I suppose someone from the family should, but to tell you the truth, it just never occurred to me. I guess I was too focused on getting Mother home before she made another scene."

"Yeah, I appreciate that. So, why'd you call, Charlotte?"

"Well, it's Mother. She, uh...she says she needs to get away for a while. So she's decided to go home with Roger and me."

"What about her job?"

"She'd already talked to the head of the university about taking an emergency sabbatical, and they're being very understanding. Midterm starts soon, so it's a fairly good time. It'll be difficult, but President

Toomy is sure he can find a substitute professor to fill in for Mother.''

''How long does she plan on being away?''

''Until the fall semester starts.''

''I see.'' Typical, he thought. His mother was going to be gone for nine months or so, but she couldn't bring herself to call and tell him herself. She had to get Charlotte to do it for her.

''I'm sorry, Dillon,'' Charlotte said softly. He didn't have to ask for what. Both of his siblings had always been aware of their mother's animosity toward him.

''Yeah, well, par for the course. Tell her I hope she enjoys her visit.''

''Uh...actually, there is one other thing.''

''Shoot.''

''She wants to know if you'll keep an eye on her house while she's away, maybe stop by every few days and water her plants and make sure everything's all right?''

Dillon gave a snort of mirthless laughter. ''Sure. Why not.''

''Oh, good. She'll be relieved. She said to tell you she'd leave the key under the mat.''

She'd have to, Dillon thought. She refused to give him a key of his own to her elegant little town house.

''So, when are you leaving?'' he asked.

''Actually...we're heading for the airport in a few minutes. We're booked on an early afternoon flight to Sarasota.''

Silence stretched out as Dillon absorbed that. He supposed he should consider himself lucky that she'd bothered to let him know at all. If she hadn't needed him to look after her precious plants, she probably wouldn't have. "I see. Well, have a good flight."

When he turned from hanging up the receiver, Emily held her coffee cup cradled between her palms and gazed out the window at nothing.

"Looks like you got a reprieve," he said, taking his seat again. "Mother is going home with Charlotte and Roger. They're flying out this afternoon."

Emily blinked and looked at him. "Really? Just like that? Without even saying goodbye?"

"Apparently." He polished off his coffee and wiped his mouth with a napkin. "Can you be ready to leave by ten-thirty?"

"Leave?"

"You have an eleven o'clock appointment to meet with your attorney. I'll drive you."

Emily groaned. "Do I *have* to? I know what the will says. Everything comes to me."

"I'm afraid you don't have a choice. Life goes on, and the first of the month is coming up."

"So?"

"So you'll have to pay bills—car payments, mortgage payment, utilities, that sort of thing. Then there's the funeral costs. Your attorney will have to file the will with the Probate Court before all the assets can be released to you."

"I suppose you're right. Oh, Lord, I have no idea where to start. Keith always handled those things."

Dillon frowned. "Are you telling me that you have no knowledge of your personal finances? How much you have? What you owe? What your investments are? Dammit, Emily, that's crazy."

"You don't have to act as though I'm a twittery fluffbrain. I did offer to take on the job after we married, but Keith insisted on turning everything over to Bob Larson. He's our tax attorney and business manager and an old friend of Keith's."

"Yeah, I know who Bob Larson is. He and Keith went through public school and college together."

Emily shot Dillon a curious look. He'd made the statement matter-of-factly, but something in his voice told her that Bob Larson wasn't one of his favorite people.

"That's right. Anyway, Keith said he didn't want me to be burdened with boring financial matters and he didn't have the time to handle them himself."

Actually, the arrangement had bothered Emily a great deal when she and Keith had first married. By then, at age twenty-two, she had been on her own for years and had been accustomed to paying bills and handling her own finances. That discussion had sparked one of the few serious arguments that she and Keith had ever had.

"Still, Keith should have kept you up to date on your financial picture," Dillon insisted.

"I know," she said wearily. "I tried to convince him of that, but whenever I brought the matter up it always seemed to anger him, as though he thought I didn't trust him."

"Well, you're going to have to jump in with both feet now. Whether you take over your finances or you continue to retain Larson, you'll need to familiarize yourself with your fiscal situation.

"Within a week or so you'll have to start dealing with whatever obligations you have. You can probably access your joint accounts, but if there are any others solely in Keith's name, neither you nor Larson can access those until the will has cleared probate."

Propping her elbows on the table, Emily dropped her head in her hands and groaned again. "I can't deal with this right now."

"You don't have a choice. Look, if it'll help, I'll sit in on the meetings with you. But this has to be handled."

Emily raised her head and found herself looking into her brother-in-law's intense blue eyes. She had never expected the time would come when she would be grateful for Dillon's company. "You'd do that?"

"Sure. That's what I'm here for."

Emily stared at the attorney in disbelief. "What do you mean, there's nothing left? There has to be. My husband was a physician with a highly successful practice."

Bob Larson shifted in his chair, and looked at her pityingly. "I'm sorry, Emily."

"But...we had investments—stocks, bonds, real estate, that sort of thing."

"All gone." Bob's mouth compressed into a grim line. "I did advise Keith not to sell off his assets. Actually, I pleaded with him, but he wouldn't listen. Over the past four years, one by one, he liquidated almost everything."

"There was a sizeable life insurance policy. What about that?"

"He cashed it in about a year ago."

"Our savings?"

"That, too. I'm afraid all you have is whatever is in your checking account."

"Oh, dear Lord." Emily sagged against the chair back, dazed. This couldn't be happening. It had to be a bad dream. Surely she would wake up soon.

But it was real. Horribly real. Her husband had not only been unfaithful, he had deceived her in other ways as well. And apparently he'd left her penniless.

"Wait a minute," Dillon said, leaning forward in his chair beside Emily. "How could Keith sell his stocks and other investments without Emily's knowledge? Wasn't she co-owner? If so, her signature would have been required, too."

"Yes, of course. And I assure you, the documents were properly signed and executed."

Dillon looked at Emily. "Did you ever sign anything for Keith without knowing what the document was?"

Emily shook her head slowly, still too stunned to speak.

"You must be mistaken, Emily," Bob insisted. "Keith couldn't have sold those assets without your signature."

"Not unless he signed her name to them himself," Dillon stated.

"Oh, I hardly think Keith would do that." Bob gave a dismissive chuckle, but a look from Dillon turned the sound into an embarrassed cough.

"Apparently he did."

Emily's stunned gaze fixed on her brother-in-law. "Are you saying he forged my name?"

"Looks like it."

She felt sick. Just when she thought she'd learned the worst of Keith, she discovered yet another layer of duplicity.

Emily felt as though she been beaten to a bloody pulp, knocked to the ground, then kicked while she was down.

"If that's the case, let me assure you, I had no

idea,'' Bob asserted. ''Had I even suspected such a thing, I would have done everything in my power to stop him.''

He drummed his fingers on the desktop and heaved a sigh. ''I hate to give you more bad news, but I'm afraid you will be held responsible for all of Keith's outstanding debts. As soon as I file the will with the Probate Court, the people to whom Keith owes money will be coming to you for restitution.''

''Yes, I know. Dillon has already reminded me to make the mortgage and car payments.''

Bob cleared his throat. ''Well...uh...I'm afraid there are considerably more debts than that. Keith has several outstanding loans.''

''He borrowed money? Without telling me?''

''I'm afraid so. Of course, I had no way of knowing that he hadn't consulted you.''

''I'd like to see those loan documents,'' Dillon said in a brusque voice. ''You do have them, don't you?''

''Well, yes, but, uh...I'm sorry, Dillon, but I can't turn them over to you. That would be a breach of attorney-client confidentiality.''

Dillon drilled him with a narrow stare. ''Your client is deceased. Emily is his sole heir and, as you pointed out, liable for his debts and obligations. I am here at her request to advise her. Now, you can either give us all records related to Keith now, or we'll get a court order. Either way, you *will* hand them over.''

Bob's mouth compressed. It was obvious that he wanted to refuse, but he couldn't quite muster the nerve. ''Very well, if you insist.'' He flipped through a thick file folder, withdrew a single sheet of paper and handed it across the desk to Dillon. ''Here is a list of all of Keith's loans.''

Dillon barely scanned the sheet. ‘‘These are just totals. I want the loan documents and every other scrap of paper pertaining to my brother. Now,’’ he added when Bob’s expression turned mulish.

For several seconds the two men engaged in a silent battle of wills, their gazes locked, but Bob Larson was no match for Dillon.

‘‘Oh, all right,’’ he snapped finally and shoved a thick file folder across the desk toward him.

‘‘I don’t understand,’’ Emily said as Dillon flipped through the folder. ‘‘Why on earth did Keith need so much money? Where did it all go? Surely he didn’t spend it all on…on that woman.’’

‘‘I’d like to hear the answer to that, too,’’ Dillon said. ‘‘And don’t try to tell me you didn’t know what was going on. You and my brother were old friends.’’ He tapped the file folder with the back of his knuckles. ‘‘And with this kind of extravagant spending you must have questioned him.’’

Bob’s face turned pink and he squirmed in his chair. Then he heaved a weary sigh, like a man about to come clean and unburden his conscience.

‘‘All right. I guess there’s no reason to keep his secrets now. I’ve known for years that Keith was doing some risky financial maneuvering—taking out high-interest, short-term personal loans to pay off credit cards and other debts, sometimes to pay off a previous loan. He was always just a step ahead of disaster—what my grandmother used to call, robbing Peter to pay Paul. He did spend a lot on women, but—’’

‘‘Women?’’ Emily gasped. ‘‘You mean there was more than one?’’

‘‘I’m afraid so. Over the years Keith had a string

of mistresses. For a time, each one occupied the town house.''

''I see.'' The words hit her like a fist to the midsection. Emily's heart contracted with pain, but she somehow managed to hold her head high.

''But that's not where all the money went,'' he continued. ''It was a combination of things, really. As I'm sure you know, your husband had very expensive taste.''

''Yes, that's certainly true.'' Their home was a prime example. From the first, Emily had thought it too large and ostentatious, and much too expensive. She had wanted to purchase something a bit smaller, but Keith had insisted that a doctor of his standing needed a showplace home.

''While he made an excellent living, Keith insisted on enjoying a lifestyle far beyond his means,'' Bob went on. ''In addition to the condo and the Lexus he purchased for his mistress, there was the beach house and the boat, expensive cars for himself and you. And there was Keith's gambling.''

''Gambling? My husband *gambled?*''

''Oh, my, yes. Last year alone he made five trips to Las Vegas. He bet heavily with local bookies, as well.''

If Bob Larson had leaped across the desk and hit her with a club Emily couldn't have been more stunned. Or more devastated.

Keith had gone on gambling trips and she hadn't even known. Thinking back, she realized that all those times he'd told her he was attending a medical convention he'd actually been gambling in Las Vegas. No doubt his mistress of the time had been with him.

Lowering her head, Emily cupped her hand over her eyes. She couldn't bear this.

"I'm so sorry, Emily," Bob said softly. "I didn't want to be the one to tell you. I tried to reason with Keith. Honestly I did. But he wouldn't listen."

She shook her head, unable to reply.

"Dammit, Larson," Dillon growled. "What kind of friend are you? You knew all about Keith's carousing and extravagance and his gambling addiction, yet you never alerted his family to the hole he was digging himself into."

"I…it wasn't my place to interfere," Bob blustered. "What did you expect me to do? Go tattling to his wife behind his back? So he was cheating. So what? That's no big deal. A lot of husbands do it. As for his gambling, that was his business."

"You should have come to me and explained what was going on. I would have stepped in." Dillon snapped the file folder shut. "Is there more we should know? Anything else you're covering up for my brother? Any other nasty little surprises?"

"Uh, no…no, that about covers everything."

"Good. Then we're done here. I'm sure you won't mind if we take this folder with us."

The other man looked as though he were about to object, but Dillon silenced him with a look. Tucking the folder under his arm, he stood and gently assisted Emily to her feet.

Normally she would have flinched when he slipped his arm around her waist, but she barely noticed. Moving like a zombie, she allowed him to lead her out of the office.

At the door, Dillon stopped and looked back at the attorney. ''By the way, your services will no longer be needed. I'll have my attorney file the will with the Probate Court.''

Chapter Three

Dillon glanced at Emily's ashen face. She hadn't spoken one word since they left Bob Larson's office. "Are you okay?"

She didn't answer. He wasn't sure she'd heard him.

She sat in his pickup on the opposite side of the bench seat, huddled in a ball of misery against the passenger door, her arms wrapped tightly around her middle. She stared straight ahead at nothing, her expression blank.

No small wonder, he thought. These past five days she'd received one blow after another.

"Emily? Emily, answer me. Are you okay?" he asked again, a little louder this time.

She started and turned her head, blinking at him. "Wh-what? Oh." Facing forward again, she replied in an emotionless voice, "Yes. I'm okay."

"You sure? You're not feeling any pain or anything, are you? Any nausea?"

This time the look she shot him held even more confusion. "What? No, of course n— Oh. Oh, I see. You're concerned about the baby." Her mouth twitched. "Don't worry. Your niece or nephew is safe. Physically I'm doing fine."

Dillon ground his teeth, angry that she'd put that interpretation on his concern, but he forced himself to speak gently. "The baby's well-being is important, but I'm more worried about you. This week has been rough."

The bitter laugh that burst from her was tinged with hysteria. "Yes. You could say that."

Dillon parked in the driveway and ushered Emily inside. He watched her shrug out of her coat and hang it in the entry closet then turn without a word and walk into the living room.

When Dillon had shed his own coat and followed he found her in the bay window alcove, staring out the window at the bleak winter landscape. She stood with her arms folded tight across her midriff, as though she feared she might fly apart at any second and was trying to physically hold herself together.

He stopped a few feet behind her. Everything about her telegraphed desolation—the angle of her head, the rigid set of her shoulders, her paleness. She looked fragile and tragic, and absolutely alone.

"Emily, we need to talk."

"Not now, Dillon. Please."

"I know you don't feel like doing this now, but it's urgent. You have to take stock, get an idea where you stand before you can make a plan."

Her upper body began to jerk. Lowering her head,

she hunched her shoulders and hugged herself tighter, but the convulsive jolts came stronger and faster. A small, choking sound tore from her throat. Then another, and another.

The hair on Dillon's nape stood on end. "Emily?"

Unable to subdue the sobs any longer, she raised both hands and covered her face, and gave in to the gut-wrenching tears she had been holding back for days.

"Aw, Emily." In two long strides Dillon closed the space between them, spun her around and snatched her into his arms. "It's okay. Everything will work out," he insisted. "You'll get through this. You'll see."

The gruff pep-talk had no effect. Clutching his shirt with both hands, she wept uncontrollably against his chest. The wrenching sobs tore from her, so raw and raspy he knew that they hurt her throat. Her entire body shook with each agonized cry.

Dillon felt so helpless. He longed to banish her pain, to shield her from all the ugliness and betrayal, but he could not. At that moment he came close to hating his brother.

Powerless to do anything except let her grief run its course, he rubbed his hands in slow circles over her back and rocked her from side to side. "That's right, let it all out. You'll feel better when you do."

His words made her cry even more forlornly. The great, wracking sobs seemed to come from the depths of her soul. They tore at Dillon's heart and made him wince, and he held her closer still, as though doing so would allow her to absorb his strength.

Finally her tears ran dry and her sobbing slowed to

watery sniffles and shudders, then to hitching little breaths.

"Oh, Dillon," she mumbled against his wet shirt. "Wh-what am I going to d-do?"

Before he could answer he heard her sharp intake of breath, and he realized that she'd suddenly become aware of their position. She stiffened and scrambled back several steps, her expression horrified. "I—I...I'm sorry. I don't know what came over me."

"I think you reached critical mass. After all that's happened, a meltdown was probably inevitable. Don't worry about it," he said in a gravelly voice. "You're entitled."

Running a trembling hand through her hair, Emily pushed the long, auburn mass back until it cascaded over her shoulder, all the while eyeing him warily.

Dillon ground his teeth. Clearly, she did not expect sympathy from him.

"Well, uh...thank you for being so understanding." Her eyes were bloodshot and red-rimmed and her eyelids puffy. Tears glistened on her cheeks and streaked her makeup. The tip of her nose was red and her face was pale and blotchy from crying. Her misery broke Dillon's heart.

"No problem. And to answer your question, you're going to get through this one step at a time. And I'm going to help you.

"The first thing you're going to do is go upstairs and wash your face, maybe take a nap." Taking her arm, he started leading her toward the stairs in the entry hall. "After that crying jag you probably need one."

"But you said—"

"I know, but I changed my mind. You're in no

shape to dive into the legalities right now. Just go get some rest. I'll take a look at Keith's financial records. When you're ready, we'll sit down and go through everything together and figure out where you stand financially."

Emily made a feeble attempt at a chuckle. "I can tell you that now. I have no money, no insurance settlement, no investments and no income."

"Yeah, well, don't worry about it," he growled. "We'll figure something out."

"We?" She stopped at the bottom of the stairs and turned.

Dillon could see her pulling herself together. Drawing in a deep breath, she squared her shoulders and tipped up that delicate chin.

"Look, Dillon, I appreciate all you've done, but this isn't your problem. It's mine. There's no reason why you should be burdened with it. I'll deal with it by myself."

"How?"

"I...I'm not sure. But I'll think of something. My point is there's no need for you to concern yourself."

"Really?" he snapped, struggling to contain his impatience. "I can think of several."

Her chin came up another notch. "Such as?"

"Such as, it's because of my brother that you're in this fix."

"So? You're not responsible for Keith's actions."

"Maybe not legally, but that's beside the point. You're still a part of this family. And don't forget, the baby you're carrying is a Maguire."

"All the same, I—"

"It's no use arguing about it, Emily. I'm going to help."

His implacable blue gaze bore down on her. She met that laser stare in silent frustration. She wanted to scream. She didn't want to be around anyone, least of all him.

She felt guilty for the thought, but it was true. Ever since she'd received the news of Keith's death, Dillon had been there for her, like a rock, offering silent support during the unpleasant meetings with the doctors and the police, making all the funeral arrangements, running interference between her and the gossipmongers. During the past four days he'd talked with her more and in gentler tones than he had in all the years she'd known him. In truth, she didn't know what she would have done without him these past few days.

Even so, he was still a tough, taciturn man. And he still made her uncomfortable.

Emily sighed. No matter how she felt, the sad truth was, she needed help. She was still reeling and too depressed and bereft to function, much less deal with legal matters on her own. And there was no one else to whom she could turn.

"All right, you win," she huffed finally.

"Good. Now why don't you go get some rest?"

She shook her head. "No. I'd rather get this over with. Anyway, I doubt that I could sleep for worrying. I'll just go up and wash my face. I'll be right back."

Dillon watched her climb the curving stairway, his gaze zeroing in on her erect posture and the proud tilt of her head.

A smile tugged at his lips as he pictured the way she'd tipped her chin up at him. The action was typical of Emily.

On the outside she was gracious and soft-spoken,

but she had a backbone of tempered steel. He had recognized that about her within minutes of their first meeting, seven years ago.

Emily was the kind of woman, Dillon mused, who in days gone by, would have stepped in without a qualm and taken over running the family farm while her man marched off to war, even if she had to plow the fields herself with a baby on her hip and a rifle slung over her shoulder.

That strength and indomitable spirit was one of the many things he had admired about her from the beginning.

Emily hadn't known that grief could be so debilitating. Or was it the anger that seethed at her core? Either way, she felt drained. Just climbing the curving stairway took tremendous effort. It was as though every cell in her body were weighted with lead. It didn't help that she could feel Dillon's laser-beam stare boring into her back.

In her bedroom she stripped off the cashmere suit she'd worn for her meeting with the attorney. Her panty hose came next. Wearing just her panties and bra, she went into the bathroom. Catching sight of herself in the mirror above the sink Emily groaned. She looked a fright. She had cried away most of her makeup and her mascara had run in streaks over her cheeks, making her look like a red-eyed raccoon.

Twisting her hair into a loose knot at her crown, she secured it with a couple of small combs and creamed away what was left of her ruined makeup, then splashed her face with cold water. As she patted her skin dry she winced at her reflection. She was so pale she looked anemic.

A dusting of powder, a sweep of blush and a quick dab of lipstick provided only marginal improvement, but it would have to do. What did it matter, she thought. The only person who would see her was Dillon, and she wasn't trying to please him.

She paused and frowned at her reflection, remembering the way he had held her close and comforted her.

Funny. She had always found his size and ruggedness intimidating, but being held against that brawny chest with those strong arms wrapped around her had felt surprisingly good. And safe. As though nothing in the world could harm her in the shelter of Dillon's embrace.

She shook her head and wrinkled her nose at her reflection. What a fanciful thought. You must still be in shock if you're starting to think of Dillon as a knight in shining armor.

She returned to the bedroom and donned a pair of casual navy slacks and a cream turtleneck sweater, slipped her feet into a pair of classic loafers and headed downstairs.

When Emily entered the kitchen, she found that Dillon had brewed a pot of coffee. Before taking her to the attorney's office he had changed into a suit. Now he'd removed his coat and tie and unbuttoned the collar and rolled up the sleeves. He sat at the table with the file folder spread open, scowling as he read. In his right hand he held a steaming mug of coffee.

Dillon looked up and arched one eyebrow as she crossed the room and poured herself a cup of coffee. "Feeling better?"

She turned and leaned her hips back against the counter and took a sip of coffee. "Not really, but I'll manage.'' She nodded toward the folder. ''How's it going?''

''I was on the phone with my foreman for a while, so I just got started. I'm going to need some paper to write on so I can total everything up as I go.''

Emily pulled a legal pad and some pencils from a drawer and sat down beside him at the table. Immediately her nose was assailed with a mixture of smells—coffee, soap, the clean, woodsy scent of his aftershave, even a hint of starch from his crisp dress shirt. And underlying it all, was that unique masculine scent that was his alone. It was not an unpleasant combination, yet it made her uncomfortable. Breathing in his scent seemed so…so intimate, somehow.

If Dillon was equally aware of her he gave no indication.

Taking the yellow legal pad, he divided it into two columns with a vertical line down the center and scrawled *Assets* at the top of one side and *Liabilities* at the top of the other.

''Okay, this first document is a short-term bank loan for ten thousand dollars that he took out just last week,'' he said, recording the outstanding balance in the liabilities column.

For the next couple of hours they went through every piece of paper and document in the folder. There were numerous personal loans with various banks around town. Most, according to Bob Larson's records, were used to pay off Keith's bookie, but in recent months it appeared that Keith had taken out loans to pay off earlier loans.

''Larson was right about one thing,'' Dillon commented tersely. "Keith was operating just one step ahead of disaster. His finances were a juggling act."

There were at least four credit cards that Emily had known nothing about, all with astronomical balances. An examination of the charges showed he'd purchased several luxury items for a woman—perfumes, jewelry, flowers, a fur—none of which had come to Emily. There were charges for restaurants and nightclubs and tickets to theater productions that she had not attended. In addition, the sailboat was only half paid for and there were the mortgages on the house, the beach house and, most galling of all, on Keith's little love nest.

When they were done Dillon's face was grim and Emily felt as though she'd been kicked in the stomach.

"Dear Lord. It's worse than I thought." She stared at the figures on the pad, feeling sick. The liabilities column stretched almost to the bottom of the page, and the total was staggering. The only items listed in the assets column were the house and her car, a three-year-old Cadillac that Keith had been badgering her to trade in on a new one for the last six months. Thank heaven she had resisted.

"Damn," Dillon spat. "What the hell was he thinking? He made an excellent living but he'd been trying to live like a billionaire."

Groaning, Emily lowered her face into her hands. "You know Keith. Self-denial was never in his vocabulary."

"Yeah. We have Mother to thank for that. She spoiled him rotten his whole life. By the time he was in his teens he was sure the world revolved around him. To tell the truth, I was amazed when he had the self-discipline to stick it out through medical school and his internship and become a doctor. If he hadn't loved medicine so much he would never have done it."

Unable to sit still any longer, Emily bounded out of the chair and started pacing the kitchen. "There's only one thing to do. I'll have to sell the house."

"Whoa. Wait a minute. There must be another way."

"Really? What else do you suggest? Our savings and investments are gone and there's not enough in my household account to make the next mortgage payment."

"What about the clinic? Surely Keith has some money coming from there."

"A half-month share in the profits maybe, but that's all. The partnership agreement states that if a partner dies, his share in the clinic is split among the other doctors."

"I see." Dillon raked his hand through his hair. "Look, why don't you let me pay off your creditors and the mortgage."

She stopped pacing and shot him a horrified look. "No. Absolutely not. I won't hear of it."

"Dammit, Emily. I can't let you give up your home. You love this place."

"Actually…I don't." She smiled wanly at his shocked expression. "Keith's the one who insisted we buy this house. He wanted something that shouted, 'I've made it.' I've never liked this house nor have I felt truly at home here. It's too big and too stiff and formal. I wanted something cozier and warmer."

"I see. The trouble is, though the value of this house has risen a good deal since you bought it, even if you sell for top dollar the profit you'll make won't be enough to pay off all of Keith's creditors."

"I'll sell Keith's Porsche, too. And the sailboat and the beach house. And if I have to, I have some jewelry I can sell."

"Like hell, you will," Dillon growled. "Before it comes to that I'll personally go to every bank that loaned Keith money and pay it back myself, whether you like it or not."

"You'll do no such thing," she snapped back. "It's my jewelry, and I'll do with it what I please. You don't have anything to say about it."

"Dammit, Emily, I hate the thought of you selling your jewelry."

"Why? I have no intention of wearing any of it ever again."

He frowned. "Why not?"

She turned to him with glacial eyes, her face set. "Because your brother gave me every piece."

Dillon stared at her, his chest suddenly tight. What did that mean? That she didn't want anything that was in any way connected to Keith? If so, did that include the baby? And him?

The latter would come as no surprise. He even expected it. Especially since she'd never been fond of him anyway. He also looked enough like Keith to be a constant, unwanted reminder of her faithless husband.

She claimed to want the baby, but had she been telling the truth? It made him sick to even think that she might reject the child she carried because she believed it was Keith's.

No. He refused to think that. Not Emily.

"I see," he said finally. "All right, then. If that's how you feel."

He picked up a document from the file. "This is the insurance policy on the condo. Luckily it will cover the cost of rebuilding. I checked."

"You can't be serious. I'm not going to rebuild that place."

"I'm afraid you don't have any choice. The covenants in that complex require that you rebuild, and the other owners will insist on it. But look on the bright side. You can probably sell it for a tidy profit."

"Fine. The sooner the better," she muttered.

"Also there's the Lexus that Keith bought for his lady friend. The loan papers on the car are in the file. It was purchased in Keith's name, which means you can sell it."

This time Emily answered with a bitter look and continued pacing.

Using a fresh sheet of paper, Dillon did some quick calculations. "If my estimates are right, if you sell everything we talked about, you may have enough to pay off all Keith's creditors, but just barely. There won't be much left over."

"It doesn't matter. Just as long as I get free of these debts." She sank back down in the chair and closed her eyes.

"Don't start feeling too relieved. You still have a major problem."

"What do you mean?"

"You and the baby have to live."

"I know," she replied wearily. "I'll just have to get a job."

"Doing what? You haven't held a job since you graduated from college and married Keith, and you never finished the work required to get your teacher certification."

"That's because Keith insisted that I stay home. He didn't want a working wife."

"I know that. I wasn't criticizing, just stating facts."

Emily sighed. "At the time Keith claimed that he wanted to spoil me and make up for the 'pillar-to-post' existence I had known for most of my life. I came to realize that he thought having a working wife would somehow diminish his status."

A bitter chuckle escaped her. "Oh, he knew just which buttons to push to get his way. He made me feel, for the first time in my life, that I was cherished and loved. So naturally I complied with his wishes and became the pampered, stay-at-home doctor's wife that he wanted. What a mistake that was."

"Yeah, I know," Dillon muttered. He had told his brother at the time that he was being unfair to Emily. She'd worked hard to become a teacher, putting herself through college with a series of menial jobs, and she deserved the chance to attain her goal. However, Keith, being Keith, had merely laughed and brushed aside his concern, saying that as the wife of a prominent doctor she would have financial security and social standing, and that was much better than being a low-paid, unappreciated teacher.

"Still, regardless of the reasons, you're not qualified to teach," Dillon persisted.

"Then I'll get a job in an office somewhere. I have a college degree. That has to count for something."

"That's true. Except you're going to find that there are few companies that will be willing to hire a pregnant woman."

"That's not fair."

"Maybe. But that's how it is."

Emily gritted her teeth and looked away. She knew he was right, but that only made her feel more helpless and angry. "I'll find something," she declared stubbornly. "If worst comes to worst, I can always go back to waiting tables."

"Don't be ridiculous!" he snapped. "You have no business being on your feet all day, hefting heavy trays of food. You have a baby to think of."

She glared at him. "Don't you think I know that? I *am* thinking of the baby. As you pointed out, we both have to eat and have a roof over our heads."

Frustrated, Dillon ground his teeth and studied her mulish expression. It was clear that he wasn't going to dissuade her about getting a job. And he knew better than to offer to take care of her, though he could easily afford to do so. She'd probably heave something at his head if he suggested it.

"All right. All right. If you're determined to do this, after you've had a few weeks to adjust and take care of personal business, like finding another place to live and selling this house, then you can come to work for me."

Chapter Four

"What?" Emily gaped at Dillon, shocked and just a tad angry. She wouldn't allow him to pay her bills, so now he thought he could just create a job for her out of thin air? Oh, no. Not on your life.

"Thank you, but no. I couldn't possibly work for you."

"Why not? I'm not suggesting that you operate a crane or rivet steel beams twenty stories above the ground. I'm offering you an office job. That way you at least won't be on your feet all day."

"I appreciate the offer, Dillon, but I won't take charity—not from you or anyone."

"What are you talking about? I'm offering you employment."

"Oh, please. Giving me a fabricated job doesn't make it any easier to take. It's still charity." And, she added silently, I don't want to be indebted to you for my livelihood.

"That's it? You think I'm featherbedding, just to provide you with a living?"

"In a word, yes. For some reason you seem to feel that you're responsible for me. Frankly, I don't understand why you would feel that way now, when for the past seven years you've barely acknowledged my existence.

"Maybe you're feeling guilty for what Keith did, or maybe it's some misplaced sense of family responsibility. Whatever the reason, I will not be a leech or a burden."

"You couldn't be more wrong," Dillon said in a voice like ice. "My on-site office assistant is snowed under with work. She's been nagging me for months to hire someone to help in the construction office."

"Then why haven't you?" she challenged.

"Because I haven't had time."

"Oh, please. Surely you have a personnel department for that sort of thing."

"That's right. But Gert's been with me from the day I started my business, so she rates special treatment. She asked me to hire her next assistant and I told her I would. She trusts my judgement a lot more than Personnel's. The site office is small and the staff there needs to be especially compatible. The last three people Personnel hired to assist Gert nearly drove her crazy. I thought she might strangle the last one."

Emily's eyes widened. "It sounds like this Gert person is the problem."

"Oh, she's plainspoken and brusque and she doesn't suffer fools for a second, but she's got a heart of gold. If Gert takes a liking to you, you've got a friend for life."

"What makes you think she'll like me?"

His vivid eyes flickered over her. "Trust me, she's going to love you. And make no mistake about it, if you come to work for me, you'll earn every penny of your salary. If you don't, Gert will boot you out of there in a New York second, just like she's done all the others."

"Now there's a comforting thought."

Dillon shrugged. "Do your job and you won't have any trouble. My point is, you'll carry your weight just like everyone else on my payroll."

The statement jerked the rug right out from under Emily. His coldness, along with the dangerous glint in his eyes told her beyond any doubt that he was telling the truth, and that left her feeling foolish. She was not, however, willing to accept defeat.

"I see," she replied. "Nevertheless, even if the job is legitimate, I still don't think it's a good idea."

"Why not?"

Because you make me nervous, she thought. *Because it would be uncomfortable for both of us. Because no matter how hard you try to make up for your brother's betrayal, I would always know that, deep down, you don't really like me.*

"It isn't good for morale," she said. "Nepotism never goes over well with other employees."

"Is that all?" Dillon threw his head back and gave a harsh bark of laughter that made her jump. "Trust me, Gert will probably give me a kiss and jump for joy, and none of the guys on the work crew will give a rat's a—uh...a rat's nose. What goes on in the office is just a bunch of paper-shuffling nonsense to those guys.''

''Still—''

''Emily, will you be reasonable?'' he demanded, exasperation beginning to roughen his clipped tones. ''Face it, in your condition this is the best offer you're going to get. I'm offering you a job that won't be detrimental to you or the baby. Allowances will be made for any special needs you may have, as they are for all pregnant women in my employ, and you'll have full benefits and earn a decent wage.''

He named the salary he was offering and she frowned.

''That seems a lot for a beginning position. Are you sure you're not inflating the salary just for my benefit?''

''Aw, hell.'' Dillon clapped his hand over his eyes and muttered a string of curses beneath his breath. It was the most emotion she'd ever aroused in him, and it left her speechless.

Slowly, he pulled his palm down over his face. ''Damn, woman, you sure make it difficult to help you. I pay top-dollar to all my employees. That's how you get and keep good people.''

She pounced on the comment with a self-satisfied, ''Ah, but you can't possibly know that I'll be good at the job. You don't even know what my skills are.''

''I know that you're bright and hardworking. You couldn't have put yourself through college if you weren't. You're honest, capable, reliable, conscientious. I also know that whatever you undertake you do a thorough job of it. As long as you have those qualities, Gert can teach you the rest of what you'll need to know. What I don't know is why you're fighting this so hard.''

Bowled over by his estimation of her, Emily was too stupefied to answer for a moment. Dillon believed she was intelligent and capable? Keith had always dismissed her achievements as unimpressive and unimportant, especially compared to his own, and treated her as though she were a not-too-bright pretty doll.

''I...that is...I—I just don't think it's a good idea for us to work together, that's all,'' she stammered.

He pinned her with a piercing stare, holding her gaze so long she had to fight the urge to squirm. ''We're not enemies, Emily,'' he said in a low, rough voice that sent a little shiver down her spine.

''I know. But we're not exactly friends, either.''

She raked her fingers through her hair again. How could she explain? She couldn't very well tell him that something—call it intuition or instinct or just a gut feeling, whatever name you wanted to put on it—cautioned her that close contact with Dillon would turn her life upside down. She didn't want that. She'd had enough upheaval in her life.

Propping her elbows on the table, Emily cradled her head in her hands. What was she going to do? There was no one else to whom she could turn for assistance. Certainly no one in her family—such as it was.

Oh, Lord, she thought with utter despair. This couldn't be happening. It was her childhood all over again.

The first eight years of her life she'd lived with her mother's elderly parents. She had no idea who her father was. Her grandparents had told her that he was a war hero who was killed serving his country, but Emily suspected that was just a story they made up for her benefit. Delia Collins had been, at best, a "sometimes" mother who had drifted in and out of her life when it suited her.

After the deaths of her grandparents she'd been shuffled from one relative to another. None of them had wanted her. Not really. Each had merely taken her in for a while out of a sense of obligation and family honor.

Emily couldn't think of a single one of her kin who would be happy to have her turn up on their doorstep again.

The hard truth was, she was alone, flat broke, unemployed and pregnant. And at the end of her rope.

"What's your problem?" Dillon asked. "It seems to me that it all boils down to two choices—you either take a low-paying, back-breaking menial job for slave wages—if you can find one—or you come to work for me."

Emily raised her head and sent him an annoyed look.

Unfazed, Dillon cocked one eyebrow. "So? What's it going to be?"

She pressed her lips together and held his gaze, torn. Finally her shoulders slumped and she released a long sigh. "Very well. I'll take the job," she replied, none too graciously.

The relief that poured through Dillon almost buckled his knees. His instinct was to wrap her in cotton wool and shield her from all harm and worries. If he had his way she would spend the next nine months doing nothing but pampering herself and anticipating the arrival of this baby that she had dreamed of having for so long.

However, the only way that was going to happen was if she'd let him support her, but he knew better than to even suggest that. At least she'd be working at Maguire Construction. That way he'd be able to keep an eye on her and make sure she was okay.

"Good. I'm glad we've got that settled," he said in his usual brusque tone. "Now we can get started on liquidating your assets."

"You mean right now?" She closed her eyes and massaged her temples. "Can't it wait a day or two? I really don't feel like dealing with this right now."

"Believe me, I hate to press you, Emily. I know you're feeling down, but the truth is, there's no time to waste." He tapped the file folder spread out in front of them. "According to Larson's records, you've got several loan payments, two car payments and three mortgage payments due within ten days, not to mention utilities and other regular monthly expenses."

She shot him an alarmed look. "What! Even if I sold the house tomorrow I wouldn't have the money by then!"

"I know. What I propose is, for the present, I'll make the payments, and you can reimburse me later."

"Dillon, I already told you I won't take money from you. It isn't—"

"Before you get all bent out of shape, let me assure you, this is just a loan. You'll pay me back out of the profits from the house."

"But—"

"It's the only way, Emily," he insisted. "You have to keep on top of these debts, and at the same time you have to eat."

Frustrated, she stared at him, grinding her teeth. He could tell that she was searching for an alternative and drawing a blank. Finally, she sighed. "I guess you're right."

"Good. Now then, the first thing we have to do is get the will filed with the Probate Court. I'll call my attorney and get him on that today."

"On such short notice?" She gave him a doubtful look. "It seems unlikely that he'd just drop everything to handle something like this."

"Don't worry. For what I pay him, he'll do it.

"The next step is to put the house on the market. You can't finalize the sale of the house or any other asset until the will clears probate. However, we can get the ball rolling and line up buyers.

"Unless you have another real estate agent in mind, I can recommend this friend of mine. Lois is a sharp cookie, and she handles mostly high-end properties like this one. She can probably get you top dollar."

"Fine," Emily replied listlessly. "I don't care who handles it, as long as I can sell it soon. I'll even include most of the furniture. I need only a few pieces to furnish a small apartment."

The sooner she could get out of this house and put all the memories and betrayal behind her, the better. In a place of her own she would start fresh and build a new life for herself and her child, with no lying, cheating man around to break their hearts.

"Good. I'll give Lois a call. She may be able to handle the sale of the beach house, too, although my hunch is we'll have to find an agent in Galveston for that. I'll also see about selling the sailboat and Keith's Porsche and that Lexus, if that's all right with you."

"Yes, of course. Do whatever you think is best."

Dillon noted her bent head, the utter desolation in her body language, and his heart clenched. Before he could stop himself he reached out and touched her forearm.

Instantly, her head jerked up.

Her startled stare saddened him. Over the years, to hide his feelings, he had deliberately kept his distance from Emily, both physically and emotionally, but in doing so he had made her defensive and wary of him. It was going to take time and tremendous effort to overcome that—providing that was even possible. After what Keith had done, who could blame her if she was leery of men. Particularly Maguire men.

He sighed and met her wide-eyed gaze with a steady look. "Emily, I know that right now you're hurt and angry and confused, and rightly so, but it's all going to work out," he said softly. "I promise."

Over the next six weeks Emily learned firsthand just what a take-charge, dependable man Dillon was.

As he had promised, his attorney, Warren Price, came to the house that very day with some papers for her to sign and took with him the original copy of the will to file with the Probate Court.

The following morning Dillon's friend, Lois Neeson, swept in on a cloud of perfume and went through the house like a blond tornado.

From the woman's attitude Emily realized that she and Dillon had once been more than mere friends, and that Lois would not object to picking up where they had left off.

Emily had known that Dillon dated a lot of women. Only the previous year one of the local newspapers had done a piece on Houston's most eligible bachelors, and he had been among the top ten. Which was hardly surprising. After all, he was a man in his prime who owned and operated a highly successful business that had made him wealthy. He was also handsome, in a rugged sort of way, and he had a steely, dangerous look about him that some women found fascinating.

However, Emily had never actually seen Dillon with a woman before, and she couldn't help but be curious about what type he preferred.

As she showed Lois around the house she experienced a prickle of distaste at the way the woman flirted with him constantly. Funny. She would never have figured that he would be interested in such an aggressive female, but she supposed there was no accounting for taste.

For his part, Dillon didn't respond to any of the woman's coy looks and innuendoes or the way she hung on his arm, but neither did he do anything to discourage her either.

Lois's appraisal turned out to be even higher than Emily had hoped it would be, so she put aside her dislike and listed the house with the agent. Business, after all, was business, and Dillon's friend was apparently sharp when it came to real estate.

The very next day Lois returned with a prospective buyer in tow, and she showed the house at least once a day after that.

The first couple of days immediately following the funeral the telephone rarely rang, and Emily assumed that people had refrained from calling out of respect. However, by the third day Dillon began receiving numerous calls—from his foreman, his office staff, bankers, suppliers and many others. Walking past the study while he was on the telephone with his foreman, Emily overheard enough to know that he was urgently needed, but Dillon refused to budge.

"Dammit, Eric, you're going to have to handle it yourself," he growled into the receiver. There was a pause, followed by, "No, I don't know how long I'll be here. However long it takes. Just do the best you can and keep me informed."

He slammed the telephone receiver down. Scowling, he turned and saw Emily standing in the doorway. At first surprise, then wariness flickered across his face before it resumed its usual remote expression.

"Go home, Dillon," she said quietly. "You've neglected your business long enough."

"It'll survive without me a while longer," he said with an unconcerned shrug. "My people know what they're doing."

"Maybe so, but you're obviously needed there more than here. I'll be fine on my own. I appreciate all you've done for me. Really, I do. But it's time for you to go back to your own life."

"That can wait," he argued. "You shouldn't be alone right now."

"It has to happen sometime. You can't stay with me forever."

He pinned her with an inscrutable stare for so long she began to feel uneasy, but finally he replied, "Maybe not, but I can be here now."

Emily exhaled a heavy sigh. She had hoped it wouldn't come to this. "Look, Dillon, I don't want to be rude but the truth is, I'd prefer to be alone. So please, just go."

He studied her expression in silence for a time.

"All right. If that's how you want it. I'll go gather my things."

Emily experienced a twinge of guilt as he drove away, but she told herself it was for the best. She was alone now, and it was time she began to deal with that. Besides, having Dillon in her home, seeing his face constantly, reminded her of Keith. His presence was like pouring salt in an open wound.

If Emily had thought that removing Dillon from her home would banish him from her daily life she soon learned otherwise.

He called her often to ask how she was and if she needed anything and to keep abreast of how things were progressing with the sale of the house. The sound of that deep, gravelly voice never failed to send a prickly sensation up her spine. In addition, three or four times a week he dropped by her house on his way home from work to help her deal with the loose ends of settling the estate and assist her with sorting through her things and packing.

Even sunk as Emily was in a pit of depression and grief, as the weeks passed she realized that in every way possible Dillon continued to do his best to take the burden off her shoulders and shield her from additional stress.

He dealt with all the tedious and unpleasant details like disposing of Keith's clothing and personal items and going through the files in his study and his desk. Dillon even cleaned out Keith's office at the clinic and collected the money owed to her. With the exception of Dr. Conn, she hadn't heard from any of Keith's partners or their spouses since the wake, though prior to that, they had all supposedly been friends.

It took almost four weeks for the will to clear probate, and by then Dillon had a buyer for both cars, the sailboat and the beach house and all the necessary paperwork had been done. It took only her signature on the documents to complete the sales.

In less than two weeks after she listed the house with Lois, Emily received a full price offer, and closing on the property occurred just a month after that.

Emily hadn't expected the house to sell so quickly, which meant she had to scramble for another place to live. All she could afford in her price range was a small, one-bedroom apartment. In this, too, Dillon came to her aid, locating a tiny, but clean place not far from his own high-rise condominium.

"The location is convenient," he explained. "It's only five minutes to my main offices on Post Oak and fifteen or twenty from the construction site. We'll be on that job for another year to fifteen months, so that'll make your commute easy."

As Dillon had predicted, it took almost the entire proceeds from the sale of the house and the other assets to retire the horrendous debts that her husband had incurred and reimburse him the money he had advanced her.

Just as she suspected would be the case, he did not want to take the money, particularly when he knew she had barely enough left to see her through another month. Nevertheless, she insisted. Over the past few weeks they may have reached a stage of mutual tolerance, but she still wasn't comfortable owing him money.

On moving day Dillon arrived early with a crew of

burly construction workers and a stake bed truck with his company logo painted on the side. They made short work of loading her belongings, and by noon Emily locked the house for the last time and followed the truck to her new apartment.

She was bent over, her head and upper body inside a large box when Dillon stepped into the kitchen an hour later and announced, "I'm going to go pick up burgers and fries for the men for lunch. What would you like?"

Emily popped up with a newspaper-wrapped bowl in her hands. Dillon's eyes widened ever so slightly, and she self-consciously straightened the long flannel shirt that hung to her mid-thighs. She must look a mess, she thought, to get even that much of a reaction from him.

Her face tingled and she knew it was red from practically standing on her head, and wispy curls had worked loose from her French braid and fluttered around her overheated face. She pushed the tendrils back and attempted a polite smile. "A burger will be fine, thanks."

He glanced around at the mishmash of items she'd already unpacked and the stacks of remaining boxes. Already, wadded-up newspaper lay a foot deep on the floor.

"Don't do any lifting, okay?" he said. "In fact, why don't you take a break? When I get back, I'll give you a hand in here."

He was out the door before she could reply.

Emily had no intention of taking a break. Having something physical to do kept her mind busy and helped chase away the depression that had been weighing her down for almost seven weeks. However, she had already realized that she'd gotten a little ahead of herself. After all, there was no point in unpacking until she'd lined the cabinets with shelf paper, otherwise she'd have no place to put things.

Kicking off her shoes, Emily climbed up on the counter to measure the top cabinet shelves.

The U-shaped kitchen was small. Within a half hour she had measured all the upper shelves on the left side and covered them with the pretty blue-and-white paper and was sidestepping over the sink to measure the ones on the right side when an explosive curse made her jump.

"What the *hell!*"

Emily let out a yelp as powerful hands plucked her off the counter.

The next thing she knew she found herself in Dillon's arms, cradled against his rock-hard chest.

Chapter Five

Emily caught her breath. Their faces were so close she could see each individual black lash that framed those startling blue eyes and the spokes of slightly darker blue that radiated out from his pupils like crystals. She felt his breath feathering over her cheek.

His scent surrounded her, earthy and warm and tinged with the smells of soap and aftershave and sweat. All along her right side she felt the rock-solid wall of his chest, and everywhere their bodies touched his heat seemed to seep into her. The intimacy of that sent a little shiver rippling down Emily's spine. Her heart hammered crazily against her ribs, but she could not pull her gaze away from those blue eyes, turbulent now with emotions she didn't understand.

What was the matter with her? She felt...strange. Sort of tingly all over, as though every nerve ending in her body had suddenly sprung to life. Even the tips of her breasts throbbed.

She licked her suddenly dry lips, and Dillon's jaw clenched. "Wh-what are you doing?" she demanded, but the croak in her voice robbed the words of the hauteur she had intended.

His scowl deepened. "What am *I* doing? What the hell were *you* doing?" he countered in a furious snarl. "Prancing around up there on top of the counter like that."

"I was *not* prancing. I was putting in shelf paper."

"Shelf paper? *Shelf paper?*" He looked away, grinding his teeth, and muttered a string of curses under his breath. When he looked back at her his jaw was so tight he could barely speak. "Of all the foolish, frivolous—dammit, woman, you could have fallen and broken your neck. Or harmed the baby. Did you think of that?"

"Oh, for heaven's sake, I'm not a clumsy ox you know. And will you please put me down," she hissed under her breath, rolling her eyes toward the open doorway between the kitchen and the dining alcove. "In case you hadn't noticed, we're being watched."

He glanced in that direction and saw that the men were sitting around the long trestle table from her former kitchen eating their burgers and fries and watching them with silly grins on their faces.

Dillon's mouth thinned. Muttering a soft "Sorry," he turned to shield her from their view and placed her on her feet. Emily took a quick step back and made a production out of straightening her shirt and smoothing the wispy curls away from her face, all the while not quite meeting his eyes.

"I never said you were clumsy," he continued.

"But, dammit, you haven't got any business climbing around up there in your condition."

"Oh, for—" Emily huffed and rolled her eyes. "What on earth has gotten into you, Dillon? I'm pregnant. I'm not an invalid. Nor am I helpless. I've installed shelf paper in cabinets many times. I know to be careful."

"Shelf paper," he spat again with disgust. "Why the hell do you need that stuff anyway? What good is it?"

Emily had learned to be self-reliant as a young child, but she'd never been particularly combative—until now. After marrying Keith she'd been so happy and grateful to finally have the kind of ideal, "all-American" life that she'd always dreamed of having that she had deferred to her husband in most things. And what had that gotten her? Well, no more. From now on *she* was in charge of her own life, and if some man didn't like it, too bad.

"It keeps the shelves sanitary and it looks nice. I happen to like it and I'm going to have it, whether you approve or not," she declared with a pugnacious lift of her chin. She was tempted to add a childish, "So there" and stick out her tongue, but she managed to restrain herself. Just barely.

However, she had gotten herself all worked up, and her emotions, which were never far from the surface these days, suddenly flared. For no logical reason, her eyes filled with moisture and her chin began to wobble.

"You're not going to cry, are you?" Dillon demanded.

His tone merely made the tears come faster. She blinked furiously, trying to hold them in check, but, one by one, they spilled over her lower lashes and streaked down her cheek.

''Ah hell. I'm sorry. I didn't mean to snap at you. Please don't cry, Emily.''

Oddly, his sudden switch to gentleness had an even more devastating effect on her emotions, and the floodgates swung open.

''Ah, c'mon, Emily. You don't want to cry in front of the men, now do you?'' Dillon cajoled softly under his breath.

She whirled and presented him with her back. Fighting for control, she gasped and sniffed and wiped her cheeks angrily. ''Why don't you just g-go away and leave me a-l-lone,'' she cried. ''I don't need your h-help. I can ma-manage the rest on my own. I don't know why you're here, anywa-way. You don't even l-like me. You don't appr-prove of me or anything I d-do.''

The more she tried to control her tears the harder she cried, and the harder she cried the more humiliated and angry she became.

''That's not true. I lo— I like you just fine.''

''See! You can't even sa-say it without choking,'' she wailed. ''Oh, just go away!''

At the mercy of her emotions, she gave up the battle, buried her face in her hands and wept like a heartbroken child.

''Ah, Emily.'' Grasping her shoulders, Dillon spun her around and pulled her into his arms. She struggled at first but he refused to let her go, and after a moment she gave up and collapsed against his massive chest, weeping piteously—for what, exactly, she hadn't the slightest idea.

Dillon held her close and rested his cheek against

her crown, stroking her back and rocking her from side to side. "Ah, Em, don't cry so," he crooned against the top of her head. "C'mon, now. You'll make yourself sick if you keep this up. Look, if you want shelf paper that badly, I'll install it for you myself."

She shook her head against his chest. "It's...it's not the sh-shelf paper."

"I know," he replied softly. "I know."

"Y-You do?"

"Sure. You've been through one helluva lot these past weeks. Now you're moving from your beautiful home into this, small, cookie-cutter apartment all alone and starting over. If that weren't enough, you're expecting a baby. Hell, that alone is enough to send anyone into a tailspin."

He paused a beat, and his voice dropped to an intimate pitch. "I've always heard that pregnancy made a woman emotional, but this is the first time I've witnessed that firsthand."

Emily's eyes popped open. He was teasing her. Dillon was actually *teasing* her. She could even swear that she'd heard a smile in his voice.

She couldn't believe it. In seven years she'd never known him to be anything but remote and stern. In the past, when he'd bothered to speak to her at all he'd been abrupt to the point of rudeness. Granted, since Keith's death he'd made an effort to be civil, but until now there had not been that gentle razzing note in his voice. Not around her, at any rate.

Pondering that, Emily frowned and blinked her tear-drenched eyes. What was he up to?

The Maguires had never made her feel like part of their family. From the first her mother-in-law had made it clear that she didn't like her—but then, Adele hadn't thought any woman worthy of her youngest son.

On the few occasions when Emily had been around Charlotte, her sister-in-law had been polite to her, but not particularly friendly. She suspected that Charlotte took her cue from Adele. But of the whole family, it was Dillon who had made her feel most unwelcome.

So why would his attitude toward her soften now?

The emotional storm, which had diminished to watery sniffs, finally quieted altogether, but she was loath to move. It occurred to Emily that she felt wonderfully safe and secure in Dillon's embrace—and comfortable.

Too comfortable, she admitted, feeling foolish.

Inhaling a hitching breath, she placed her palms flat against his chest and stepped back. As Dillon's arms fell away Emily felt a chill but she ignored the little shiver that rippled through her.

Sniffing, she wiped her cheeks with her fingertips. "I'm sorry. I don't know what's the matter with me. I feel like such an idiot." She grimaced at the wet blotch on the front of his chambray shirt. "And I got your shirt all soggy."

"No problem," he replied quietly. He stood with his feet braced wide, his arms crossed over his chest, watching her intently.

Was he worried that she was going to dissolve into tears again at any second? If so, Emily couldn't blame him. During the past seven weeks she'd wept all over him twice. Considering that he'd never seen her so much as shed a tear in the seven years he'd known her, he was probably concerned that she was on the verge of a breakdown.

A wan smile tugged at Emily's mouth. No doubt he was worried about what he'd do if she was. He felt obliged to look after his brother's widow, but she doubted he would be thrilled to be stuck with an unbalanced female.

"You okay now?"

"Yes. You were probably right. Most likely it was just my hormones running amok. Nothing to worry about."

"Good." He picked up the roll of shelf paper from the counter. "Now...since you want those shelves lined so badly I'd better get started."

"No, Dillon, I'll do it. Really, I insist. I can't expect you to do everything for me. I'm on my own now. I have to accept that and start fending for myself."

"Maybe so, but humor me on this, will you?"

"But—"

"You wanna come show us where you want this stuff, Mrs. Maguire?"

Both Emily and Dillon turned to see Eldon standing in the doorway. The dining alcove was empty and the table had been cleared of all take-out debris. The men had finished eating and returned to work without either her or Dillon noticing.

Billy Ray and Hammer were at that moment toting her solid cherrywood Philadelphia highboy through the living room, and J.C. was right behind them with the headboard of her four-poster bed.

"Go on, and show them how you want things arranged," Dillon ordered, reverting to his usual gruff tone. "I'll give the men a hand unloading the rest of the stuff. We can finish up in here and put things away after they're gone."

The men finished unloading by midafternoon. No sooner had they left than Dillon set to work in the kitchen.

By seven the kitchen floor was knee-deep in bubble wrap and wadded newspaper and cluttered with empty boxes, but everything was put away and her pretty cobalt-blue glass canisters were lined up on one of the counters and wicker baskets of various sizes and shapes sat atop the cabinets. Dillon had even hung her collections of copper molds and blue-and-white Delft plates on the walls.

Emily looked around. The place still seemed cramped and unfamiliar, but at least with a few of her things in place it wasn't quite so cold.

Dillon began gathering up the debris and stuffing it into the empty boxes, and Emily pitched in. When they were done he announced, "As soon as I take this stuff out to the Dumpster I'll go pick us up something for dinner. After we've eaten we'll tackle the rest of the boxes."

"Thanks, but that's okay," she said. "The kitchen and bathroom are done and my bed has clean sheets and blankets on it. The rest can wait until tomorrow."

"You sure?"

"Yes. I'm tired. If you don't mind, I think I'll just open a can of soup for dinner then take a shower and go to bed." Actually, she doubted she would even bother with food at all. In the last half hour she had begun to feel the now familiar queasiness churning in her tummy.

She didn't know why it was called morning sickness. For the last four weeks she had experienced bouts of nausea at all hours. Once the vile sensation had awakened her out of a sound sleep.

Dillon looked her over. ''Yeah, you're probably right. You do look a little peaked. You've done enough for one day. I'll be back in the morning to help you finish up.''

''Oh, no. Please don't bother. I can handle the rest myself. Anyway, it's easier for me to put things away than to show or tell you where they go. There isn't that much, and I have all day tomorrow to finish.''

Dillon eyed her again, and Emily felt her skin prickle under that intent stare. Finally he nodded. ''Okay. If that's how you want it.''

He made several trips to the Dumpster with the filled boxes. On his last he stopped by the door and fixed her with another long look.

Lord, he made her nervous, Emily thought. Just being near him made her insides flutter.

Praying she wasn't turning green, she laced her fingers in front of her, forced down the bile rising in her throat and waited for him to leave.

''So, I'll see you at the site office on Monday, right?'' he asked finally.

''Yes.''

''Good. I'm afraid you'll have to spend the morning filling out paperwork and taking a physical at Keith's old clinic. My insurance company insists on that. Usually either Dr. Young or the other family practice man act as our company doctor, but maybe in your case it would be better if you saw Dr. Conn.''

''I'm sure that won't be a problem,'' she said, straining to hold on to her pleasant expression. ''I'm due for a checkup next week, anyway.''

He nodded. ''Then I'll have Gert set it up that way as soon as she gets in Monday morning.''

Emily waited in frantic silence, swallowing hard

against the rising sickness, but still he did not budge. She was certain that at any second she was going to disgrace herself, but at last he said, ''I gave you directions to the construction site, didn't I?''

Emily nodded, not trusting herself to speak. Her hands knotted into fists at her sides, so tight her fingernails dug into her palms.

''Okay, then. Office hours are eight to five. If you want to make points with Gert, I suggest you be there a little early. She doesn't tolerate lateness. And trust me, you don't want her on your case. When riled, she's hell on wheels.'' He stuffed his Stetson on his head and opened the door. Emily gratefully sucked in a deep gulp of the frosty air that rushed in. ''I'll see you Monday morning. Be sure and lock this door,'' he tacked on and stepped outside.

As the door closed behind him Emily leaped forward and turned the lock, then sprinted for the bathroom with her hand over her mouth.

When the awful sickness passed she rinsed out her mouth, brushed her teeth and washed her face. Carrying the wet washcloth with her, she stumbled out of the bathroom and sank down on the edge of her bed. She still felt queasy, a sure sign that, at a minimum, she was in for an unpleasant few hours. These episodes were either over with one quick up-chuck or they lingered for hours or even days, coming at her in waves.

Great timing, she thought despondently. Nothing like showing up the first day on a job sleep deprived and looking like something the cat dragged in.

Emily turned her head slowly, her gaze taking in the strange room with its stark white walls and ugly vertical blinds covering the window. A jumble of unopened boxes still cluttered the cheap beige carpet. She sighed. The place had all the appeal and warmth of a barracks.

She pressed her lips tightly together to hold back another silly rush of tears. Well, she thought. This was it. This was the beginning of her new life.

Though she'd been a widow for nearly two months, she'd spent all that time cleaning up the mess Keith had left her and tying up loose ends. Now all that was behind her. As of today, she was starting over.

She glanced around again. How ironic. This place looked a lot like the one she'd lived in while she'd struggled to put herself through school.

Emily gave a little snort, and a wry smile wobbled on her lips. After seven years of being a dutiful wife and helpmate, she was right back where she'd started. Her marriage to Keith had been just a colossal waste of time.

Well...except for this one precious gift he'd given her, she thought, pressing her hand against her lower belly.

With a groan, she fell over onto her side and curled into a ball and waited for the next wave of sickness to claim her.

On Monday morning, with Dillon's advice ringing in her ears, Emily left her apartment early, but even so she was very nearly late.

The shopping mall that his company was building was on the west edge of Houston in an area surrounded by new homes and businesses. The site covered several acres but it was currently little more than an enormous stretch of concrete amid a sea of rough, bare ground, and she drove right past it. By the time she realized she had gone too far and doubled back she was running short of time. Finally she spotted the Maguire Construction Company sign and turned into the site behind an enormous concrete truck.

Scattered across the site were two gigantic cranes and numerous other pieces of heavy machinery that she couldn't identify. There were also several temporary structures that resembled long metal boxes set on concrete blocks, but nothing that looked like an office to Emily.

Off to one side a cluster of vehicles, mostly pickup trucks and a few battered old clunkers that seemed to be held together with Bondo and rust, formed a parking lot of sorts, and more were arriving all the time.

Pulling up next to a pickup where a man in a hard hat was unloading his tool box, Emily rolled down her window and called, "Excuse me, but could you tell me where I could find the office?"

The man turned away from the tailgate, effortlessly holding the enormous tool box in one hand, his bicep bulging to the size of a grapefruit. He was about Dillon's age and wickedly handsome, and when he spotted her his eyes sparked with male interest. "Why yes, ma'am. It's that first one over yonder on your right."

"Thanks."

"Is there something I could do for you, Miss?" He put down his tool box and sauntered over, giving her a sexy grin as he braced a hand on the top of her car and leaned down to get a better look. "My name's Grady Williams. I'm one of the crew bosses on this job."

Emily blinked at him. The men in her and Keith's social set had been doctors and other professionals.

Several had flirted with her, to be sure, but they had been more sophisticated and subtle about it. It had been years since Emily had been faced with this kind of bold male, and she was out of practice.

"Uh, thank you, but no. I, uh…I just needed to find the office. Thanks for pointing me in the right direction."

With what she hoped was a polite but dismissive smile, she turned her car toward the white metal structure he had pointed out and drove away. In the rearview mirror she saw the man watching her, standing with his hands planted on his hips and a wide grin on his face.

Emily shook her head. Keith's behavior had left her feeling unloved and undesirable. If nothing else, working for Maguire Construction was going to be good for her battered ego.

The big clock on the office wall registered one minute before eight when Emily stepped inside. There was no sign of Dillon, but the gray-haired woman behind the first desk glanced up. For an instant, Emily thought she saw shock flash in her eyes, but it was gone before she could be certain.

She was so nervous her insides were quivering. It had been almost ten years since she'd started a new job.

She had risen at five and washed and blow-dried her hair and taken extra pains with her makeup. For her first day on the job she had dressed conservatively in an elegant navy suit and cream silk blouse, but one glance at the other woman's casual slacks and sweater told her that she'd overdressed. Strike one, and she'd barely gotten her foot in the door.

"Good morning," she said, striving for composure. "I'm Emily Maguire."

"I figured," the older woman acknowledged with a brisk nod. "Dillon said you'd be starting work this morning. Not a moment too soon, either, I don't mind telling you. He insisted on holding the job for you, so I've been putting up with incompetent temps for the last two months."

"I, uh...I'm sorry."

Gert waved aside her apology. "Wasn't your fault. I know you had some grieving to do. I just hope you're going to be an improvement. I'm Gert, by the way. Gert Schneider."

"I figured," Emily replied, unable to resist tossing the woman's words back at her.

Gert's head came up sharply. Emily tipped up her chin and met her gaze without flinching. She was not by nature a rebellious or aggressive type, but neither was she anyone's pushover.

Gert cocked her head to one side and eyed Emily with new interest, her gaze trailing over her from her auburn hair to the toes of her expensive Italian pumps, then back again. "You know, I had my doubts about you. But I can see now that I was wrong."

"Oh really?" Emily cocked one eyebrow in unmistakable challenge. "What sort of doubts?"

The other woman hesitated, eyeing her. "You sure you want to hear this? I'm warning you, I'm a plain-spoken woman."

"By all means, please continue."

"Well then, to tell you the truth, I figured you for a well-to-do lady who enjoyed her pampered lifestyle so much she turned a blind eye to her husband's cattin' around and wastrel ways."

It was the most stunning insult that Emily had ever received. She felt betrayed all over again. "I see," she said with frosty dignity. "I take it he filled you in on my husband's dirty secrets."

"Who, Dillon?" Gert snorted. "Lordy, child, you must not know him at all if you think that. That man's as closed-mouthed as they come. You'd have about as much luck prying personal information outta him as you would the Sphinx.

"Anyway, it wasn't necessary. The newspapers were chuck full of gossip about that doctor husband of yours and his mistress and their cozy love nest, and how they were found nekked as two jaybirds when it went up in flames."

Emily winced, but her expression remained impassive. She had not read a newspaper for weeks after Keith's death. She couldn't recall even seeing one around the house during that time. It occurred to her then that Dillon had probably intercepted them to keep her from seeing the hurtful articles.

"As for the rest," Gert continued in her steamroller fashion, "I figured the only reason you'd go to work at all is because you need the money, which can only mean that sorry husband of yours had frittered away everything."

"I see."

"But I've changed my mind, leastways about you. You're a little bitty thing and you look about as sturdy as a buttercup, but danged if you don't have gumption." She looked her up and down again. "Yessiree, I do believe you'll do just fine."

"Thank you very much. That's so nice to know," Emily replied, but if Gert caught the dry note in her voice she didn't let on.

"Now then," Gert continued in her no-nonsense tone.

"The insurance company insists that every new employee get a physical before starting work. Dillon left instructions for me to schedule an appointment for you with Dr. Conn." Gert slanted Emily a curious look. "I've never sent anyone to him before. We've always used the two G.P.s as our company doctors, either Sanders or Weston. Dr. Conn must be your personal physician at the clinic."

"Yes. Yes, he is."

"Hmmm. Well, anyway, I've set up a nine o'clock appointment for you. As soon as you've filled out these employee forms you'd best be on your way." Handing her the papers, Gert waved toward the only other desk, which Emily assumed would be hers.

By the time Emily finished filling out the forms the older woman was on the telephone, chewing out some hapless soul about a missing order of something called rebar. Emily took the opportunity to check out her surroundings.

The office that she and Gert were to share was located in the center and took up two thirds of the long trailer. It was plain as could be, with white walls of some sort of fiberboard and a gray linoleum floor. The room contained the usual assortment of office equipment—two desks, each with its own computer, a printer, filing cabinets, copy machine, fax machine, and a drafting table. In a corner was a tiny kitchen area with a sink, coffee machine and a small, under-the-counter refrigerator.

At one end of the room an open door revealed another office, which Emily assumed was Dillon's. At the opposite end another door sported a discreet little sign that read Rest room.

Not the most plush of offices, Emily thought, but it was functional and probably very practical, as it could be moved from one job site to another.

Though she'd never seen it, she knew that Maguire Construction's main office was located on Post Oak Lane in a plush high-rise that Dillon's company had built, but she had a hunch that this plain, utilitarian box suited her austere brother-in-law more.

Just as Gert ended her tirade and slammed down the telephone receiver the outside door opened and Dillon stepped inside. Instantly the office walls seemed to close in on Emily.

Dressed in jeans, a chambray shirt, denim jacket, work boots and hard hat he looked even bigger and more imposing than usual. His large frame seemed to fill the small space.

His gaze immediately locked on to her. "Emily. Sorry I wasn't here when you arrived, but there was a little problem with a concrete delivery that I had to handle."

"That's all right. I wasn't expecting any special treatment," she stressed emphatically for Gert's benefit. She could just imagine what his assistant would say if she thought that she did. "Anyway, Gert was here. We've, uh...we've been having a talk."

"And you're still here? Amazing." His gaze switched to the other woman, and though his granite expression never wavered there was an unmistakable softening in his demeanor and a teasing light entered his eyes. "Usually this starchy old woman scares the bejesus out of new recruits."

"I do nothing of the kind," Gert flared back, but

the protest lacked heat, and Emily could see that she enjoyed the banter.

"Don't you believe her. She ran off every temp worker the agency sent us. Five minutes on the receiving end of that sharp tongue and every one of them turned tail and ran."

"Dillon Maguire, you big fibber. Five minutes, my eye. They all stayed longer than that. One lasted three weeks."

"Now there's a record."

"Humph. Good riddance, if you ask me. Bunch of inept, lollygagging goldbricks, that's all they were. I can't abide slackers or airheads," she tacked on, sending Emily a quick warning glance.

Dillon's attention switched back to Emily. "So, when is your physical?"

"At nine." She reached for her purse and stood. "Actually, I should get going if I'm going to make it on time. I'll, uh…I'll see you later." She scurried out the door, aware of his intense gaze boring into her back.

When the door closed behind Emily, Dillon went to the window and watched her climb into her car and drive away. His gaze followed the metallic-gold Cadillac as it bumped across the uneven ground, then turned onto Westheimer Boulevard.

"Does she know?" Gert asked quietly.

Reluctantly, Dillon pulled his gaze away from Emily's car as it was swallowed up by the unending stream of traffic. He looked at his assistant and blinked, only then registering the question. "Know what?"

"That you're in love with her."

Chapter Six

"What? Don't be ridiculous." Dillon looked away, unable to meet Gert's eyes and lie. "Where did you get a crazy idea like that? I'm not in love with Emily."

"Oh, c'mon. This is me you're talking to. I've known you for twenty-six years. Why, from the time you and my boy were just little squirts the two of you were practically joined at the hip. You spent more time at our house than you did your own. I've bandaged your scraped knees, dried your tears when you were hurt and paddled your bottom when you needed it. You're as much my son as Jeremy was. Trust me, I can read you like a book."

It was true. His family had moved in next door to the Schneiders when Dillon was seven. Jeremy had been the same age, and the two of them had quickly become inseparable best friends.

Dillon had also been irresistibly drawn to Gert's earthy motherliness, and the noisy, loving atmosphere in the Schneider household. Throughout his childhood and teen years his friend's home had been a haven for him, an escape from his mother's coldness and barely concealed animosity.

Adele had not cared for Gert or her husband Carl. She had thought them beneath her—intellectually and socially—but she hadn't objected to Dillon's close friendship with them. Probably because it kept him out of her hair.

Dillon's father, Colin Maguire, a college professor like his wife, had been less judgmental, but his had been a far less dominant personality than Adele's. He'd also been a ladies' man and a charmer like his younger son, and, beyond providing for his family, he paid scant attention to his two sons.

Gert had been more of a mother figure to him than Adele had ever been. After Jeremy was killed at age nineteen while serving in the army, she had turned all her motherly attention on Dillon.

At an early age Dillon had learned to keep his feelings to himself. Any show of hurt or anger on his part merely annoyed Adele and made her lash out at him all the more, and if Keith so much as suspected a soft spot in his armor he zeroed in on it. Gert had been the only person in whom Dillon could confide his deepest feelings, his hurts, his hopes and dreams.

Even so, he had never told her of his love for Emily, and he wasn't comfortable doing so now. "Yeah, well, this time you're wrong."

"Horsefeathers," Gert retorted. "You ought to see the expression that comes over your face when you look at her. If ever I've seen a man in love, it's you."

"What?" Dillon gasped, shooting her a horrified look.

"Take it easy. Emily hasn't noticed. Nor has anyone else, for that matter. I'm probably the only one who would, and that's just because I know you so well."

Shaken, Dillon closed his eyes. All these years he'd been so certain that he'd hidden his love for Emily from everyone—except perhaps Keith. He should have known that he couldn't fool Gert.

How long would it be before Emily became aware of his feelings? he wondered, experiencing a sick sensation in the pit of his stomach. For the past seven years he'd managed to hide his love for her by simply avoiding her whenever possible and remaining aloof when he could not.

Now she would be here, working in his office five days a week. *Dammit, you should have thought of that before you hired her,* he silently berated himself.

Sighing, Dillon rubbed the back of his neck. It was too late now to take back his offer. Besides, she needed the job.

And he needed her to be here where he could look after her.

"So?" Gert prodded. "Are you going to admit it or not?"

"I told you, there's nothing to admit," Dillon replied.

He went to the coffee bar and poured himself a mug of coffee. As he sipped the brew, Gert braced her elbow on her desk, propped her chin on her palm and eyed him thoughtfully.

"It's too bad Keith met her before you did," she

mused. "The two of you would have made a terrific couple."

"Actually, he didn't. At least not by much."

As soon as the words were out of his mouth Dillon could have bitten his tongue. He hadn't meant to reveal even that much. "Look, could we just drop this?" he said irritably and stalked toward his office.

In a flash Gert was out of her chair and hot on his heels. "No, I don't think we can," she said to his back.

When Dillon sat down at his desk she plopped herself down in one of the chairs facing him, folded her arms over her chest and fixed him with her sternest, "we're going to get to the bottom of this" glare.

Dillon rolled his eyes. "Don't you have work to do?"

"Of course I do, but you need to talk about this. God knows you've held it all inside you far too long already. I always suspected that you'd fallen hard for someone who broke your heart, and you'd never gotten over her. I just never imagined it was your brother's wife."

"And I never knew you had such an active imagination. Just how did you come to that conclusion?"

"It wasn't difficult. For heaven's sake, for years I've watched beautiful women throw themselves at you. You never gave any of them a tumble."

"Oh, I wouldn't say that."

Gert shot him a disapproving look. "I'm not talking about casual sex, young man, and you know it. You're a man with a man's needs, and though I don't approve, I suppose I can understand that some itches have to be scratched. But just because you took a few of those women to your bed doesn't mean anything.

Not one of them ever touched you on any deep level.''

Her voice dropped and softened with understanding. ''I knew there had to be someone who had a hold on your heart. Someone who, for some reason, you couldn't have. Behind that stony attitude you show the rest of the world, I know there's a man with a great capacity for love—too much to go through life never falling for any woman.''

For several tense seconds she simply looked at him, her eyes silently daring him to deny the charge. It was a tactic she had used on Jeremy and him many times. As kids they'd called it her ''X-ray stare,'' and had been halfway convinced that she could see inside their heads and read their minds. That steady stare had never failed to elicit a babbled confession of whatever shenanigans the two of them had been up to.

Though Dillon knew better now, he still could not hold that challenging gaze for long. Grim-faced, he looked away and sighed with defeat.

''Oh, all right. You win. I'm in love with Emily. I have been from the moment I met her over seven years ago. Satisfied?''

''Not quite. Why don't you tell me about it? How, exactly, did you meet?''

Dillon groaned and rubbed both hands over his face, but he knew it was futile to resist. Gert was like a terrier. Once she got her teeth into something she never let go.

''One day I dropped by the hospital to have lunch with Keith. Emily had checked her mother into the hospital that morning, and she'd met Keith just a few minutes before when he'd examined Delia.''

"Her mother had cancer?"

"Yeah. Funny," he mused, staring thoughtfully into the distance. "From what I've gathered, Delia Collins wasn't much of a mother. Yet, even though she had neglected her daughter all of her life, when she developed breast cancer, it was Emily to whom she turned for aid and comfort."

Dillon shook his head. "Emily was only twenty at the time and still in college, but she looked after her mother faithfully until she died. Go figure."

"Hmm. Well, as you know, no matter how poorly you're treated, blood ties are strong. Just look at you and Keith. I wouldn't exactly say he was a great brother to you, but you were always there for him, weren't you?"

"Yeah, I guess you're right," he admitted ruefully.

"So finish your story."

Dillon gave her a dry look, but it did not faze Gert.

"I found Keith and Emily in the hospital cafeteria, consulting over a cup of coffee. When he introduced us she took my breath away. If he hadn't been there I would have asked her out on the spot."

"But he'd seen her first and beat you to it."

"Not exactly. At first he didn't even seem particularly interested in Emily as anyone other than the relative of a patient. But—"

"Let me guess," Gert said, holding up her hand to stop him. "He realized that you were attracted to Emily, so naturally, he jumped in and swept her off her feet before you had a chance to."

"Something like that," Dillon admitted. "I tried not to show that I was interested in her, but Keith must have sensed it."

"If that isn't typical," Gert spat with disgust.

"Yeah, well, that was Keith," Dillon murmured, sounding a lot more detached than he felt.

Thanks to their mother, Keith had grown up believing that the world focussed on him and his needs and wants. Adele had seen to it that her younger son got whatever his heart desired, but that had not been enough for him. Keith's narcissism had included a sly, almost sadistic streak, though their mother had always labeled it healthy competitiveness.

All of their lives, even when the object in question was something that did not particularly interest Keith, if he so much as suspected that Dillon wanted it, he snatched it up for himself before Dillon could claim it—be it the last cookie in the cookie jar, a toy or item of clothing, or, later in life, a girl.

It had been a game to Keith, and with his good looks and charm, wooing females away from his intense, often somber, older brother had been easy.

Though irritating, the latter had never created a serious rift between the two of them, mainly because Dillon hadn't been in love with any of the females in his life...until Emily.

In any case, Dillon knew that getting irritated or upset merely spurred Keith on so he learned to swallow his anger. Whenever he had truly wanted something he'd hidden his emotions behind a facade of indifference. The day he met Emily he hadn't been quick enough, however, and Keith, sensing his interest, had pounced.

"Anyway, after that, she became Keith's girlfriend, and later his wife. And that was that."

"Why, that—I can't believe he actually married her just to keep you from having her," Gert fumed. "That's low, even for Keith."

"To be fair, I think he did come to love her. At least, as much as he was capable of loving someone other than himself."

Dillon suspected that Keith had also recognized Emily's longing for the stable home life that she'd never had, and he'd zeroed in on that vulnerability and used it to his advantage.

Knowing his brother, he'd probably figured she'd be so grateful to have her dream realized that she wouldn't make waves or be too demanding. From Keith's perspective that made her the perfect wife, and an up-and-coming young doctor needed a wife—an attractive, gracious wife—to create the perfect image.

It was an uncharitable thought that made Dillon feel guilty, but it was one he'd never quite been able to shake.

"So, does Emily know how you feel?"

"No. Absolutely not." Dillon jabbed his forefinger in Gert's direction, and skewered her with his stare. "And I want to keep it that way. Understand?"

Her chest puffed with indignation. "And just when have I ever betrayed a confidence of yours, I'd like to know?"

"Never, but I want to make sure you realize that I'm serious about this. So don't go dropping any hints, okay? It would be extremely embarrassing for both Emily and me if she found out and make for an uncomfortable situation around the office."

"I guess I can understand that," Gert conceded. "It is a bit soon after losing her husband."

"There is that, but I don't mean just for now," he stressed emphatically. "I don't intend for her to ever find out."

''What? Why that's crazy. She's a young woman. Give her some time to get over her grief and everything that happened, and she'll be ready to give love another try. It might as well be with you.''

Dillon gave a cynical snort. ''Trust me, that's not going to happen.''

''Why not?''

''For one thing, she's my brother's widow. After what he did I doubt that she's going to be interested in men any time soon, particularly not one named Maguire.''

For another, she's pregnant, he added silently. *Plus, she can barely tolerate being in the same room with me.* He didn't dare tell Gert either of those things though. It wasn't his place to announce Emily's condition, and if he revealed that she disliked him Gert would react like a mother grizzly protecting her cub. The last thing he wanted was to turn her against Emily.

''Oh pooh,'' Gert scoffed. ''Emily seems like a perfectly intelligent young woman to me. She wouldn't hold what Keith did against you. You two were nothing alike. I've always known that, and I'm sure that she does, too.''

''I'm not,'' Dillon replied, but his mouth twitched as he recalled how quickly Gert had sized up the differences between him and his brother.

In the beginning Keith had tagged along whenever Dillon had escaped next door to his friend's home. However, in the Schneider household Keith had not been the center of attention as he'd been accustomed to being at home. Gert had refused to treat him like a royal little prince, the way Adele did, nor would she tolerate his tantrums and demands, and Keith had soon stopped associating with Dillon and Jeremy and adopted Adele's disdainful attitude toward their neighbors.

"If you ask me, you're being foolish and pig-headed," Gert insisted. "I say, if you love the woman, go after her. Before someone else snatches her right from under your nose again."

"It's not that simple. There is more to it than you know. Things that I'm not at liberty to divulge, so don't bother badgering me about them," he added before she could question him. Swivelling in his chair, he plucked a roll of blueprints off the credenza and spread them out on his desk, giving her an arch look from under his dark eyebrows. "Now, do you think we could get some work done around here?"

"Fine," Gert snapped. "If that's the way you want it." Rising to her feet, she sniffed huffily and headed for the door. Once there, however, she paused and looked back. "Just bear in mind that Emily is a young, beautiful woman. And other men aren't blind like some I know." With that, she flounced out.

Dillon stared at the empty doorway. Letting the blueprints reroll, he leaned back in his chair and swivelled around to look out the window.

In the distance a cement truck sat disgorging its load of wet concrete, while more trucks formed a line behind it, waiting to do the same. Workmen in hard hats and rubber boots spread the gray glop over the grid of iron rebar that filled the wooden forms, adding yet more sections to the enormous foundation. Dillon automatically counted the number of trucks and assessed his crew's efforts, but his mind was occupied with Gert's tart warning.

That Emily might become romantically involved

with some other man had not occurred to him, and the possibility did not sit at all well. Just the idea of it made him want to slug something or somebody. Hard.

Nor had he given any thought to wooing her himself—at least not consciously. He'd been too busy looking after her and trying as best he could to ease her pain and straighten out the mess his brother had left to allow himself to go down that road.

Or maybe he'd just been afraid to think about that possibility. God knew, he wanted Emily in his life. He'd give everything he owned to be able to love her openly and have her love him in return.

However, he knew that before that could happen first he had to tell her the truth about the baby she carried.

Though riddled with guilt about his part in the deception, he would have kept silent had Keith lived, but not now.

On some level, he'd known since he first learned of Keith's death that he would have to tell her the truth, but he'd pushed the matter aside because he hadn't wanted to face it.

Jaw clenched, Dillon slammed his fist down on the arm of his chair. *Damn you, Keith,* he raged silently. *Damn you for creating this mess.*

Dillon groaned and pinched the bridge of his nose. No doubt, his brother was looking down right now, laughing his head off at the fix he was in.

Ever since Keith married Emily he'd seemed to take great delight in throwing her and Dillon together whenever he could. He had then sat back and smiled at their stiffness toward one another, even though Emily had not seemed to enjoy their encounters any more than he had.

No. No, that was not completely accurate, Dillon thought. Excruciatingly painful as it had been to be near her, he treasured every moment he'd ever spent in her company.

Over the past seven years his feelings for his brother had teetered between love and hate, he admitted to himself. Never more so than during the last year.

Shortly after entering medical school, Keith had confided in him that he was sterile. Dillon had assumed that he had told Emily about his inability to father children before they married. It was, after all, the honorable thing to do. However, when Emily began to talk about starting a family he'd realized that his brother had withheld that information from her.

The first chance he got he confronted Keith, for all the good it had done. Unconsciously, Dillon's hands balled into fists at the memory of Keith's reaction.

His brother had flatly refused to tell Emily the truth and had laughed off Dillon's anger with an unconcerned, "Don't worry. She'll eventually accept that it's not going to happen and forget about it. It's no big deal."

Keith's callous disregard for his wife's feelings and wishes had made Dillon see red. It had taken every ounce of restraint he'd possessed not to smash his fist into his brother's face.

"It is to her," he'd ground out through clenched teeth.

"Okay. Then I'll give her a baby," Keith replied with a shrug. "There's more than one way to go about it, you know."

Assuming that he was referring to adoption, Dillon had let the matter drop.

As he had suspected would happen, Emily did not give up hope. To Dillon's fury, Keith allowed—even encouraged—her to go through all sorts of tests and procedures, knowing all the while that their failure to conceive lay with him.

Then, just when Dillon thought his brother couldn't sink any lower, Keith had asked him to donate sperm, which he would present as his own for an in vitro procedure.

Dillon shook his head at the memory of that conversation. At first he'd been incredulous, then livid, but his fury had not touched Keith.

"Where's the harm?" he'd countered. "We share the same gene pool. Hell, we even look alike. Emily will never know the baby isn't mine."

"I won't be a part of this," Dillon had snarled back. "I don't know how you can even ask me. Dammit, how can you do this to her?"

"Hey, I'm giving her what she wants," Keith replied with maddening nonchalance. "Anyway, who are you kidding? You can't tell me that you wouldn't love for Emily to have your baby."

He had come close to hitting him then, Dillon recalled bitterly.

But Keith hadn't been finished.

"Look at it this way, it's either you or an anonymous donor." A sly grin spread over his face, and he added softly, "C'mon, Dillon. Do you really want Emily to bear some stranger's child?"

"Dammit, Keith—"

"Look, you don't have to give me an answer right now. Think it over for a few days and let me know what you decide. Just bear in mind that, one way or the other, it's going to happen.''

Dillon's teeth clenched at the memory. He had seethed for two weeks. At one point he'd come close to going to Emily and telling her the truth himself, but in the end he hadn't been able to bring himself to disillusion her that way. Especially since he wasn't certain she would believe him. Emily was nothing if not loyal.

He'd told himself over and over that he wouldn't do it, but Keith, having cleverly zeroed in on his feelings for Emily, had known just which button to push. In the end Dillon hadn't been able to stomach the thought of Emily carrying a stranger's child, innocently believing it was her husband's. He knew also that she would hate the idea.

Finally, with a mountain of misgivings and regrets eating away at him, he had given in, and on the appointed day he'd shown up at the hospital.

Now the woman he loved was pregnant with his child, believing it had been fathered by the husband who had betrayed her.

And somehow, some way, he had to tell her.

Dillon groaned. What a helluva mess.

If he had any hope of building a future with Emily, he had to start out right, and that meant having no dark secrets between them, but he had a gut feeling that telling her the truth would kill any slight chance he had of winning her.

Still, he had to try. There were plenty of men out there who would be willing to marry a beautiful widow, even if she came with a child.

His child.

Dillon's jaw clenched and he shot out of his chair

and stalked out of his office. "I'll be over at the site if you need me," he growled to Gert as he stormed through the outer office and jerked the door open.

He slammed the door behind him and cleared the steps in one leap. With a face like thunder, he strode toward the line of cement trucks, his long legs eating up the ground. The workers he passed took one look at him and cautiously gave him a wide berth. Dillon was so focused on the angry dialogue going on in his head he barely noticed them.

It wasn't going to be easy, but he'd be damned if he would sit idly by and let someone else steal the woman he loved and his child. Not again.

Chapter Seven

The door opened and Dillon burst into the office like an enraged grizzly bear. He looked so intimidating that Emily quickly ducked her head.

Following him at a cautious distance came Eric Thompson, the general foreman, Grady Williams and Hammer, all looking nervous and wary.

''Gert, call the architect and tell him to get out here. Now,'' Dillon barked on his way into his office.

Though it was almost eleven, it was the first Emily had seen of him all morning. He didn't so much as cast a glance her way, but Grady made a quick detour by her desk.

''Hiya, gorgeous,'' he murmured, flashing a sexy grin. ''How's it going?''

The flirtatious gleam in his eyes flustered Emily, and she felt hot color rush to her cheeks. ''I, uh...''

''Grady!''

Emily jumped and Grady winced. They both looked up to see Dillon glowering at them from the doorway to his office. "Mrs. Maguire has work to do, and so do you. Now get in here!"

"Sure thing, boss." Grady darted her a regretful look, but his eyes still twinkled. "Sorry, darlin'. Gotta run. I'll catch you later."

Emily watched him amble away and into Dillon's office as though he hadn't a care in the world, the fingertips of both hands stuck into the back pockets of his tight jeans.

She could feel Gert watching her and glanced her way, but instead of averting her gaze, the older woman continued to boldly study her as she spoke on the telephone and scribbled on a notepad. When Gert hung up the phone she tore the top sheet off the notepad and stood, but her gaze remained fixed on Emily. "Is there something going on between you and Grady Williams?"

Emily gaped at her, appalled. "Of course not. It's barely been four months since my husband died. Grady was just being friendly, that's all."

"Friendly, my eye. Child, if you really believe that all I can say is you've been out of circulation too long. Grady's a flirt who flits from one woman to the next. Mind you, he's a nice enough guy, if all you want is a fling, but if it's a soul mate you crave you'd do better going for more substance and less flash. Someone honest and steady and dependable. A man with a strong character and a good heart."

Oh sure, Emily thought. The only man she knew who fit that description was Dillon.

The instant the thought went through her mind she

caught her breath and her heart rate kicked up a notch. Dear Lord, where had that come from?

"Thanks, but I'm not looking for either."

The older woman shrugged. "Just food for thought."

"Gert! Get in here."

Gert pursed her lips. Taking her time, she picked up her steno pad, rose and strolled to the door to Dillon's office. "You bellowed?" she drawled.

Fighting the urge to laugh, Emily caught her lower lip between her teeth and turned her attention back to the stack of delivery receipts she'd been sorting when Dillon and the other men burst into the office.

At first she'd been leery of Gert. From the things that Dillon had told her she had expected to be at the mercy of a fire-breathing dragon lady. True, Gert ran a tight ship and there was no denying that she was abrupt and plainspoken—sometimes shockingly so—nor did she take any guff from anyone. The men on the work crew teased and joked with her, but they also minded their manners and their language in her presence—or they got the sharp edge of her tongue.

However, over the last two months Emily had gradually come to realize that Gert was also loyal, tenderhearted and motherly, in her own brusque way.

Emily had been stunned to learn that Gert had been mothering Dillon since he was seven years old. The way she praised him and pointed out his virtues, you would almost think she *was* his mother.

Gert's opinion of Dillon had come as a surprise. Not only had Emily never thought of him in such glowing terms, Dillon had always been such a loner she'd simply never suspected he would inspire that kind of love and devotion.

She supposed it said something about his character if he'd earned the support of a salt-of-the-earth type like Gert.

Now, to Emily's surprise, it appeared as though she, too, had somehow earned the older woman's loyalty. For some reason, like an old broody hen, Gert had decided to take her under her wing and treat her as her own. Given the sporadic mothering Emily had received as a child, she did not mind in the least.

A wry smile tugged at her mouth as she stapled two receipts together. Several of her preconceived notions had been shaken these past months, starting with this job. Working for Dillon was turning out a lot better than she had expected, she had to admit.

It had taken less than a week for her to realize that she had been foolish to worry that he was just being charitable and creating a job for her. There was plenty of work for her to do. So much that it amazed her that Gert had managed on her own for any length of time, even if all she'd done was keep up with what was absolutely necessary.

Emily's concerns about working with Dillon were also proving groundless. He was so busy she saw little of him.

He preferred to spend his time at this site, but there were other construction projects that demanded his attention, as well as meetings with bankers, attorneys, prospective clients and suppliers, all of which took place at his main offices. She supposed there were also administrative matters and decisions that he handled while there.

Some days she didn't see him at all, though he always called Gert two or three times a day to check on things.

Even when he was on the site, Dillon spent a great deal of time with the work crews, and she saw him only at a distance or when he dashed in and out of the office. Rarely did he stop to talk to either her or Gert, but then, Dillon had never been one for idle chitchat.

Funny, his silence didn't bother her as it once had. It wasn't so much that he was cold or distant, she had come to realize. It was just that he was either extremely busy or preoccupied with the myriad details connected with running his business.

None of the Maguire men were slackers. For all his faults, Keith had loved medicine and had been a dedicated physician, just as his father had been an excellent professor. However, of all of them, Dillon worked the hardest. In the last two months she had learned just what a huge amount of responsibility rested on his shoulders—much more than she'd ever imagined. Literally hundreds of people counted on him directly for a living.

Emily began to wonder, a bit sheepishly, if that had been the problem all along, that she had mistaken Dillon's silence and preoccupation as hostility toward her. Also, after seeing how hard he worked and how busy he was, she began to feel guilty that he had taken so much time away from his business to help her.

Gert came out of Dillon's office looking preoccupied. "Have you seen the Emerson Ironworks file?" she asked, pawing through the clutter atop her desk.

"It's in the cabinet. It was in that huge stack of folders that I filed yesterday, remember?"

"Huh. No wonder I couldn't find it. It's where it's supposed to be," Gert joked as she opened the file drawer and started walking her fingers along the tabs.

Emily glanced at Gert out of the corner of her eye, her curiosity getting the better of her. "Dillon certainly seems in a foul mood today," she commented.

In the time she had worked there she had learned that, though he was straightforward and commanding, often to the point of being abrupt, he was usually fairly even-tempered. This was the first time she'd ever seen him so riled.

"Mmm. He's got a right to be, I reckon. He just discovered a major structural error in the blueprints. If he hadn't caught it before the building went up it would have collapsed within a year. Then a few minutes ago a wall frame they were erecting fell and injured two men. He's just sent them both to the hospital in an ambulance."

"Oh, dear. How badly were they hurt?" She and Gert had heard the siren, but they hadn't paid it any mind. Westheimer, the street that bordered one side of the site, was a main thoroughfare, and emergency vehicles often went by.

"Luckily, they appear to be fairly moderate injuries—a bad cut and a broken leg. But it could have been a lot worse. And as if all that weren't enough, the fools over at Emerson's just delivered a truckload of the wrong size girders. Ah, here it is," she said, pulling a thick file folder from the drawer.

"I hope everything turns out all right," Emily said.

"It will. Dillon will see that it does."

Gert returned to Dillon's office and Emily went back to sorting receipts. She was still at it an hour later when the door opened again and an attractive brunette woman stepped inside.

Surprise trickled through Emily. The office had plenty of visitors—delivery people, salesmen, inspectors, people from the main office, from the bank and the insurance company, the city works department—but other than a couple of female truckers this was the first time since she'd been working there that a woman had dropped by the site.

And this woman, dressed to the nines in a figure-hugging pink linen suit and three-inch navy heels looked as out of place as a ballerina in a junkyard.

"May I help you?" Emily asked politely.

The woman halted abruptly and gave Emily a cool once-over. "And who might you be?"

"Me? I...I'm Emily. I work here."

"Really? What happened to the old harridan who used to run this office?"

Flabbergasted, Emily blinked several times before she found her tongue. "If you mean Mrs. Schneider, she's still in charge of the office. However, she's busy at the moment. Is there something I can help you with?"

"Hardly. I'm here to see Dillon Maguire. Is he in?" she asked glancing toward his office. The question was superfluous, as the sounds of heated male voices inside the room could be heard plainly through the open door.

"Yes, he is, but—wait!" Emily yelped when the woman took a step toward Dillon's office. "I'm sorry, Miss, but you can't go in there. Mr. Maguire is in a meeting right now and doesn't want to be disturbed." She crossed her fingers on the last, hoping it was true.

The brunette stopped and sent Emily a scathing look, but after a moment she turned back. "Very well. I'll wait."

"Um...is Mr. Maguire expecting you?"

Ignoring the question, the woman sat down in one

of the two chrome and vinyl chairs across from Emily's desk, which was the closest thing the site office had to a waiting room. With sinuous grace, she crossed her long legs and smoothed the short skirt over her thighs.

Her long, manicured nails were a couple of shades darker than the cotton-candy pink suit, Emily noted. She glanced at her own nails, trimmed short and unadorned, and sighed. It had been months since she'd had a manicure. That was only one of many luxuries she'd been forced to give up in the last four months.

For a few moments the woman looked around the office, but when that became boring she opened her purse, withdrew a long cigarette and placed it between her lips. After lighting up, she dropped the gold lighter back into her purse, took a long, lung-filling drag and slowly blew out a stream of smoke.

At the first whiff Emily felt the familiar sickening quiver in the pit of her stomach.

Oh, no, she wailed silently. It had been almost two weeks since she'd suffered through a bout of morning sickness, and she'd thought the wretched spells were over.

Thankfully, so far the episodes she had during working hours had been mild and she'd managed to conceal her discomfort from Gert and Dillon. The way her stomach was beginning to churn, however, she very much feared that she would disgrace herself if the woman did not extinguish the cigarette soon.

"Uh, excuse me, but would you mind not smoking?" she asked politely, forcing a friendly smile.

The brunette sent her a haughty look. "Yes. As a matter of fact, I would." Still holding Emily's gaze, she took a deep drag and blew the smoke directly toward her.

Emily's stomach roiled.

"She asked you nicely," Gert snapped, stomping out of Dillon's office. "And I don't blame her. Haven't you heard about the dangers of secondhand smoke, Miss Rogers?"

"Oh, please. You nonsmokers are so whiny and self-righteous."

Gert dumped the file folder she was carrying onto her desk and turned to confront the woman again, but when she glimpsed Emily's face her frown deepened. "Why, child, you look positively green. Are you all right?"

"I…" Raising her head, she stared helplessly at Gert and tried to stem the gorge that rose in her throat. "I think I'm…" Her stomach lurched. "Oh, dear."

Gagging, Emily clamped her hand over her mouth, shot to her feet and raced for the bathroom.

"Emily!"

"What the hell is going on out here?"

"Ah, darling, there you are," the brunette cooed, springing to her feet to intercept Dillon when he stormed out of his office.

He glanced at her and did a double take. "Eileen! What are you doing here?"

"Surprised?" She threw her arms around him and planted a kiss on his lips, but before she could deepen the embrace he grabbed her shoulders and pushed her away.

She pouted prettily, but Dillon was unmoved. Damn, he didn't need this, on top of everything else.

"I've been in the Caribbean for three whole months. Aren't you glad to see me?" Eileen tried to slide her arms around his neck again, but Dillon firmly removed them.

"Not now, Eileen." His gaze shot to his assistant, who was hurrying toward the bathroom as fast as her considerable girth would allow. "Dammit, Gert, answer me. What's going on?"

"Emily is sick," she snapped over her shoulder.

"Sick! What do you mean, sick? Sick how?"

"Darling, really—"

"Shut up, Eileen," he snapped.

"Well! I never—"

Dillon hurried after Gert, his long stride quickly overtaking her.

Curiosity drew Grady, Hammer and Eric out of Dillon's office. "Something wrong, boss?" Eric asked, but Dillon barely heard him.

"What do you mean, sick how?" Gert snapped. "She's pukin' her guts out sick, that's how. Haven't you got ears?"

They stopped at the bathroom door, and Dillon grimaced at the unmistakable sounds of retching coming from the other side. "What's wrong with her? What caused this?" he demanded frantically. Without waiting for a reply he whirled away. "I'll go call an ambulance."

"Oh, for heaven's sake, calm down." Gert grabbed his arm before he could take a step. "Haven't you ever heard of morning sickness?"

"Morning sickness?" he repeated stupidly. He glanced toward the closed door, then looked back at Gert. "So...she, uh...she told you about the baby."

"She didn't have to. I've got eyes, don't I? And by the way, since it's obvious that you've known all along, you might have told me."

"It wasn't my place," he said in a distracted voice, wincing again when another crescendo of retching sounded on the other side of the door. "Shouldn't I at least call her doctor? Surely this isn't normal."

"It is when someone blows smoke in your face." Gert's mouth flattened, and she tipped her head toward Eileen Rogers, who was watching them with undisguised impatience. "Emily asked her to put out her cigarette, but Miss Rogers wasn't in the mood to accommodate her."

Dillon's gaze snapped to Eileen, his black eyebrows bristled together in a scowl that made the men hovering at the opposite end of the office shift their feet and look away. Eileen blew out a stream of smoke and gave Dillon a come-hither smile.

"Why don't you go take care of that little matter while I see to Emily," Gert suggested, and opened the bathroom door and stepped inside.

Lowering his chin, Dillon headed for the brunette, eating up the distance in four long strides.

"Well, thank goodness I finally have your attention. I got back from the Caribbean yesterday, darling, and I wanted to surprise you— Oh!"

Dillon snatched the cigarette from between Eileen's fingers, stubbed it out on the sole of his work boot and flicked it into the trash can.

"Why did you do that?" Eileen demanded, looking at him as though he'd lost his mind.

"Can't you see your damned cigarette smoke is making Emily ill?"

"Really, darling, all that fuss over the hired help?"

Dillon's jaw clamped so tight a muscle in his cheek wriggled. Without a word, he grabbed Eileen's upper arm and marched her past the gaping men and out the door.

"Dillon, wait! What are you doing? Have you lost your mind?" she sputtered as she wobbled down the metal steps in her pricey three-inch heels.

He was so angry he was seeing red, and in no mood to answer. Ignoring her constant shrieks and the way her high heels sank into the dirt and made her stumble, he hauled her over the uneven ground to her snazzy little silver Porsche.

"What are you doing? No, wait!" she squawked when he opened the door and stuffed her inside. "What are you *doing?*"

"You're leaving."

"But...but I came to take you to lunch."

"You picked a helluva day for it."

He slammed the door shut and with one hand braced on the top of the car, bent over until they were almost eye to eye.

"Dammit, Eileen—"

Biting off the angry words, he stared into her startled eyes and ground his teeth, so frustrated he felt as though the top of his head were about to blow off. After a tense moment his head drooped forward until his chin touched his chest. "Aw, dammit!"

"Dillon? Darling, what's wrong?"

She hadn't a clue, he realized. Not a clue.

He wanted to give her the blistering dressing-down that she deserved. But how could he? She wouldn't understand. He could see in her eyes that she hadn't the slightest idea why he was so angry.

Eileen had been born to money and privilege and raised to think of mere workers as unimportant. Expecting her to have a social conscience and some consideration for others was like expecting a peacock to worry about a sparrow.

"Go home, Eileen," he said wearily.

"But what about lunch?"

"Not today."

"Later in the week, then?"

"We'll see."

She brightened instantly. "I'll call you tomorrow and we'll set something up."

"Fine. You do that." He straightened and thumped the top of her car with the flat of his palm. "Now, go."

Dillon stood with his fists propped on his hips and watched her drive away. Why the devil had he ever asked her out in the first place?

Boredom, most likely, he admitted. God knew, she wasn't his type.

They had gone out only a few times when he'd decided to break off the relationship. However, before he could Keith had died, and after that he'd been so tied up with the estate and helping Emily that he hadn't had time for Eileen.

She hadn't been happy about that and had taken off to the Caribbean in a snit. He supposed she'd thought she was punishing him, but to be honest, he'd forgotten all about her until today when he'd walked out of his office and spotted her.

Dillon rubbed the back of his neck tiredly. When she called he would meet her for lunch, but only to tell her that he wasn't going to see her anymore.

He turned to go check on Emily and saw that the men had followed him outside and were watching from a few feet away.

"Whooie! That's one fine-looking fox, boss."

"Shut up, Grady," Eric growled as Dillon approached them. "Don't you ever think about anything but women?"

Unfazed, Grady grinned. "Not if I can help it."

Hammer snickered and Eric shot him a disgusted look before turning his attention to Dillon. "You through with us, boss? If so, these two yahoos can get back to work—that is if Romeo here can get his mind off the ladies long enough—and I'll go see how the men are coming along cleaning up that accident."

"Go ahead. Except you, Grady. I want to have a word with you."

The other two men shot Grady identical "now you're in for it" looks and took off.

Tucking his hard hat under one arm, Grady raked his fingers through his thick shock of blond hair and asked affably, "What's up, boss?"

"Stay away from Emily."

Grady gave a startled laugh. "What?"

"You heard me."

"Look, Dillon, on the job you may be the big boss, but you got no say over my personal life."

"I do when it comes to Emily. She's my brother's widow."

Grady shifted his feet and assumed a cocky stance. "So? It's been…what? Five…six months since her husband died?"

"Four."

"Even so, four months is a long time. She's bound to be feeling kinda…you know…"

Dillon's eyes narrowed. Grady grinned.

"…lonely."

"I'm warning you, Grady. Stay away from her."

"Why?" he asked, his tone changing from amused

to challenging. "So you can have a clear field?" Grady glanced across the enormous cleared site to where the silver Porsche still sat waiting to merge into the heavy traffic on Westheimer. His gaze slid back to Dillon. "What's the matter, boss, isn't that classy brunette enough for you?"

Rage rose up inside Dillon in a hot tide. He tensed, his hands bunching into fists at his sides. "Watch it, Williams," he growled. "One more remark like that one and you're going to be spitting out teeth."

For a moment Grady seemed to actually consider taking up the challenge, but not being stupid he quickly backed off that idea. Though he was in excellent shape, Dillon was bigger and tougher and he outweighed Grady by a good fifty pounds. "If that's not it, then what's your objection? I know she's your brother's widow and you feel responsible for her, but hell, man, lighten up. Emily is an adult. She can make her own choices. Anyway, it's not like she's your sister or anything. So what's wrong with me romancing her? I'm single. She's single—"

"She's also four months pregnant," Dillon snapped.

"*Pregnant!*"

Dillon instantly regretted blurting out the information. It wasn't his place to do so. Still, it was worth the guilt just to see the look on Grady's face. He actually paled and took a hasty step back.

"That's right. After all Emily's been through and now a baby on the way, she's vulnerable, and I won't stand by and let some playboy like you take advantage of her."

"Hey, you don't have to worry about me, boss," Grady quickly declared. Shaking his head, he held both hands up, palms out and backed away another step. "I mean Emily's a real looker an' all, and I like her a lot, but a baby? Wow, that's serious stuff. And...well...the truth is, I'm just not cut out to take on another man's kid. Not even for a little while."

Sure as hell not mine, Dillon thought. "I figured."

"Listen, boss, thanks for telling me. And trust me, you can put your mind at ease. From now on, Emily is strictly off-limits. And don't worry, I'll spread the word among the other guys, too."

Dillon studied his face in stony silence for a moment. Finally he nodded. "Just so we understand each other."

"All done?" Gert asked.

"I...I think so." Emily raised her head from the commode, and Gert handed her a paper cup of water. After rinsing out her mouth she tossed the cup in the trash can and tried to stand.

"Here now, don't be in such a rush. You're so wobbly you're going to fall flat on your face if you don't sit a minute." Lowering the lid on the toilet seat, Gert pressed Emily down onto it, then wet some paper towels and handed them to her. "Here. Wipe your face with these."

Emily buried her face in the cool wetness as Gert leaned back against the sink and folded her arms beneath her ample bosom. "So...when are you due?"

Emily's head jerked up. "He told you, didn't he?"

"Who, Dillon? Nope. He didn't say a word. He didn't have to. I'd have to be blind or stupid not to notice. Once you've had a child yourself you know the look." Hooking her forefinger under Emily's chin,

Gert tipped her head up and smiled tenderly. "Anyway, child, you're positively blooming."

A wry attempt at a smile twitched Emily's mouth. "Wilting is more like it."

"Don't worry. The sickness will pass soon. I'm surprised it hasn't already. So how far along are you?"

"Just four months."

Gert's stunned expression drew a wan chuckle from Emily. "I had trouble conceiving. I had in vitro four days before Keith died."

"I see. Did he know that it took?"

Emily closed her eyes and pressed her lips together. Unable to speak for the sudden rush of emotion choking her throat, she nodded.

"Why, that—" Gert snapped her mouth shut. When she had her temper under control she continued. "I might have known. Mind you, I don't like to speak ill of the dead, but I have to say, I'm not surprised. Even as a boy Keith was a self-centered little hedonist. So don't you go thinking he was unfaithful because of anything you did, you hear me.

"Keith was like a spoiled child in a candy store grabbing whatever he wanted." Gert shook her head. "It always amazed me that he and Dillon were brothers. If they hadn't looked so much alike I would never have believed it."

"Yes, you're right," Emily agreed in a dispirited voice. "The funny thing is, for years I actually believed that of the two of them, I'd gotten the better man."

Gert snorted. "Not hardly."

"I know that now. Since I've been working here I've begun to see Dillon in a new light. He's...he's different than I thought. More caring. More...human."

Emily sighed and wiped her face again. "When I first married Keith I was so blinded by love that I didn't see him for what he really was. If I had I wouldn't have married him."

The instant the words were out of her mouth Emily shook her head and splayed one hand over her barely thickening belly. "No, that's not true. Regardless of what he did, I don't regret marrying Keith. How could I, when he gave me this precious child?"

A knock sounded on the bathroom door, and both women jumped.

"Emily? Are you okay?"

Gert rolled her eyes. "C'mon, let's get out there before he knocks the door down."

Emily grimaced, but she rose. Feeling foolish and embarrassed, and painfully aware of how washed-out and awful she looked, she ducked her head and followed Gert out the door.

She had hoped to scoot right by Dillon and return to her desk, but she should have known he wouldn't let her get away with that. When she tried he grasped her forearm and halted her.

"Are you all right?" he asked in a gruff voice. Scowling, he examined every inch of her face. "You look like death warmed over."

Gert rolled her eyes. "Why you silver-tongued devil, you. If you're not careful you'll turn her head."

"I just meant—"

"That's okay, Dillon," Emily said in a listless voice. "I know what you meant. But I'm feeling better now. Honestly."

"Nevertheless, you're going home for the rest of

the day. After that bout of sickness you have to be feeling weak as a kitten.''

''Oh, no, that's not necessary. I'm okay. Really I am.''

''Yeah, right. Just look at you. You're so pale chalk wouldn't leave a mark on you. And so weak you're trembling.''

''That's just the aftermath of being sick. It'll pass in a minute and I'll be fine,'' she asserted. At least she hoped so. Crossing her fingers, she sent up a quick prayer that this spell would be a short one. ''Really. All I need is to sit down for a minute.''

''Lie down, you mean. You're going home, Emily, and that's that.''

The thought of curling up in bed and taking a long nap did hold appeal. For the last few months she'd been so fatigued most days she felt as though she could sleep the clock around, and the sickness just added to her exhaustion.

However, she felt it was her duty to stay.

''Dillon, that's nice of you, but I can't leave Gert to cope on her own all afternoon.''

''What nonsense,'' the older woman huffed. ''Why, I've run this office alone for months at a time. I can certainly do it for one more afternoon. Anyway, Dillon is right. You need some rest. Now go along with you, child.''

Emily's shoulders slumped. Trying to resist both of them was pointless. ''Oh, all right. I'll go.''

She went to her desk, retrieved her purse from the bottom drawer, and took out her keys, but when she turned she was startled to find Dillon standing right beside her.

''Oh!'' she gasped.

Ignoring the alarmed exclamation, he grasped her arm. "C'mon, I'm driving you home," he announced, and started to steer her toward the door.

"No, wait! That isn't necessary. I can drive myself."

"Forget it. You're in no shape to drive."

"But I'll need my car tomorrow," she objected.

He snatched the car keys out of her hand and tossed them to Gert and ordered, "Have a couple of the men drop her car off at her apartment when they get off work. And call Eric on his cell phone and tell him he's in charge for the rest of the afternoon."

"Will do," Gert replied, giving Emily a smug look.

"Dillon, this is ridiculous," Emily wailed, trying to dig in her heels.

He stopped abruptly and thrust his face down until it was just inches from hers.

Emily looked into those vivid blue eyes, and her heart flip-flopped. They swirled with emotions she couldn't decipher and seemed to shoot blue flame.

"Now listen up," Dillon snapped. "I'm the boss here, and what I say goes. I'm driving you home, and that's that. Now you can either accept that gracefully and walk out under your own steam, or I'll carry you. It's entirely up to you. Either way works for me."

Emily's eyes widened, and she sucked in her breath. "Y-you wouldn't dare."

"Try me."

She stared into those turbulent blue eyes, reading the steely resolve there, and her heart began to beat in a snare-drum roll. "Oh, very well," she snapped finally. Lifting her chin she headed for the door.

Chapter Eight

On the drive to her apartment Emily sat with her arms crossed and uttered not a word. Nor did she look in Dillon's direction. However, if she'd hoped to punish or annoy him it was a wasted effort. He didn't seem to notice.

Which was just as well. Her tight-lipped silence may have started out as annoyance, but before they had driven a mile the motion of the truck had set her stomach to churning again. From that point on she remained quiet in the hope that he wouldn't notice her distress and she could escape into her apartment before she embarrassed herself yet again.

By sheer will she made it through the drive, but the instant Dillon brought his pickup to a halt in the parking lot she gave an anguished moan, bailed out of the truck cab and raced away with her hand clamped over her mouth.

"Dammit, Emily!"

Vaguely, she heard Dillon's barked exclamation and the slam of the truck door. He caught up with her as she was being sick in the flower bed just outside the entrance to the building.

When done she remained bent over, gasping for breath. If she hadn't felt so wretched and weak she knew she would have been mortified, but at that moment she simply didn't care.

"Here, take this," Dillon ordered in a gentle rumble. A dark, masculine hand thrust a snowy white handkerchief in front of her face.

"N-no, I couldn't—"

"Take it."

Lacking both the strength and the will to argue, she did as she was told. No sooner had she wiped her face than he lifted her in his arms as though she weighed no more than a block of Styrofoam.

"Oh please, you don't have to do this," she protested. "I can walk. I'm feeling much better now."

"For Pete's sake, for once can't you just accept my help graciously?"

Her mouth compressed. "Maybe I could if it were me you were concerned about, but the only reason you're being nice to me is because of the baby."

"Is that what you think?" He shouldered open the glass door and strode into the apartment lobby. As they reached the elevator the doors opened and an elderly, blue-haired lady stepped off. Dillon murmured a polite greeting and carried Emily into the cubicle.

"Well, it's true, isn't it?" Emily replied when the doors closed and shut out the old woman's startled stare.

Dillon turned his head. For a moment his blue eyes locked with hers, blazing with an intense emotion she could not quite decipher. Emily's heart tripped, then took off at a gallop.

The elevator pinged, and Dillon broke eye contact and shrugged. "The child *is* a Maguire."

Emily blinked at him, her throat suddenly so tight it felt as though she'd swallowed an apple whole. She hadn't realized how much it would hurt to have her suspicion confirmed.

For the briefest moment she was torn between tears and anger, but both required too much energy. With a resigned sigh, she swallowed her hurt and looked away. From the corner of her eye she noted the set of his jaw and knew he was furious.

Fine. Be angry, she thought listlessly. If he resented taking time away from the job, it was his own fault. She hadn't asked him to bring her home. Or to play nursemaid.

Inside the apartment, Dillon carried her straight through to the bathroom, where he washed her face with a cool cloth, then stood by while she rinsed her mouth and brushed her teeth, all the while looking as though his face had been carved out of stone.

When Emily finished he helped her into the bedroom, tossed back the bedspread and covers and eased her down on the edge of the bed.

"Hold on a sec," he ordered. He crossed the room, rifled through her dresser and returned with a clean nightgown.

"Do you need help getting undressed?"

Jogged out of her lethargy by the question, she clutched the nightgown to her chest. "Certainly not," she said with as much indignation as she could summon. However, despite her hauteur, she felt scalding color flood her neck and face.

"Fine. If you need me, just holler. I'll be in the next room."

"Dillon."

He stopped and cocked an eyebrow.

"Uh, thank you for bringing me home. Regardless of your reason, I do appreciate it. But there's no need for you to stay. I can manage now. I've been having this sort of sickness off and on for months."

"What?" He shot her a blistering look. "Why the hell didn't you tell me?"

She blinked back at him owlishly, confused by the question. "Why would I do that? I had no reason to tell you."

His jaw clenched so tight a tiny muscle in his cheek spasmed. If anything, he seemed even angrier. "No, I suppose not," he grated. "But like it or not, I'm staying until I'm sure this round of sickness has passed. So just put your nightgown on and get into bed. I'll be back in a few minutes to check on you."

For several seconds after he'd gone Emily clutched the nightgown to her chest and stared at the closed door. Why was he so angry? she wondered. And why, when it was obvious that he could barely tolerate her company, did he insist on staying? Strangest of all, why did she feel so relieved that he was?

Resisting the urge to curse a blue streak, Dillon stalked into the kitchen. He snatched up the telephone, punched a series of numbers and waited impatiently.

"Family Medical Clinic. May I help you?"

"I want to speak to Dr. Conn."

"I'm sorry, sir, but the doctor is with a patient at the moment. May I have him call you when he's finished?"

"I don't give a rat's behind if he's with the Queen of England. You tell him Dillon Maguire is on the phone and I need to speak to him about Emily. Now."

"Oh. Yessir. Of course, Mr. Maguire. If you'll just hold..."

There was a click, then canned music filled his ear. Dillon raked his fingers through his hair and shifted impatiently from one foot to the other.

"Dillon. What's up? The receptionist said you needed to speak with me, and that it was urgent."

"It's Emily."

The doctor's voice sharpened instantly. "What's the problem?"

In bald terms Dillon explained that she had been violently ill twice in less than an hour. "This can't be normal," he insisted. "I've never seen anyone so sick."

"Well...it's a little late in her pregnancy for morning sickness, I'll admit, but it's not unheard of. If she's not feeling better by tomorrow have her come in."

"Tomorrow!" If Dillon could have reached through the telephone line he would have grabbed Dr. Conn by the throat and shaken him. "Dammit, man, she's sick now! Can't you do something for her?"

"Well, if she throws up again you could try giving her a little tea and crackers afterward. That might help settle her stomach."

"That's *it!* Tea and crackers? Emily is sicker than a Missouri mule and all you do is suggest tea and crackers? Isn't there some medicine you can prescribe? Maybe an injection of something? I can take her to the emergency room if necessary."

Dr. Conn chuckled. "Take it easy, Dillon. I know being a surrogate father isn't easy. Especially for a bachelor like you. But take my word for it, there's nothing to worry about. This is perfectly normal. It's all part of the master plan."

"If that's true the master plan stinks. Emily is going through hell."

"I know. Tell her to hang in there. This stage will soon pass. In the meantime, try the tea and crackers. Oh, and once her stomach settles, tell her she should stick to a light diet for a day or so."

Dillon hung up the telephone and cursed again. Furious, he filled the whistling kettle with water and put it on to boil, then searched through the cabinets until he found a tin of teabags and a package of crackers. He also found a small ceramic teapot covered in an overall pattern of tiny, soft red roses.

He paused and examined the china pot, turning it over and over in his big hands, his expression softening. It looked like something Emily would have—beautiful, dainty and exquisitely feminine.

He had just added boiling water to the tea in the pot when the telephone rang. Muttering a curse, Dillon snatched the receiver from the wall-mounted kitchen phone, hoping the electronic chirp hadn't disturbed Emily.

"Yeah?"

There was a moment of silence. "Dillon? Is that you?"

"Yeah, Charlotte, it's me."

"I must have dialed the wrong number. I meant to call Emily."

"You didn't misdial. You reached Emily's."

"I see," she replied in a voice that said she didn't see at all. "What are you doing there? And in the middle of the afternoon at that?"

"Emily got sick at work and I brought her home a few minutes ago. She's resting now."

"Emily is ill? What's the matter with her?"

Dillon hesitated. Had Emily told his mother and sister about the baby yet? He didn't think so. Charlotte or Adele would have mentioned it by now.

Not that he'd spoken with his mother much since she'd gone to Florida. He talked to his sister every couple of weeks, but most often whenever he called, Charlotte gave him some excuse why their mother could not talk to him just then—she was out or she was asleep or she wasn't feeling well. Dillon could tell from the guilty tone in his sister's voice that they were merely excuses—transparent ones, at that. He didn't blame Charlotte. Dillon knew his mother too well for that.

"Hard to say," he replied. "She may have eaten something that upset her stomach. Or it could be one of those twenty-four-hour bugs," he lied smoothly. "Who knows?"

"I see. Well, tell her I hope she's feeling better soon."

"Sure. Anything else?"

"Actually…I'd like to talk to you. Mother is out, so I can speak freely."

"Okay, shoot."

"You should know she's absolutely livid about Emily selling Keith's house and going to work. We just found out about that a few weeks ago. Emily said that she thought you had told us, so she hadn't bothered to mention it before when we talked. I must say, it came as a shock.''

You would have known sooner if you kept in better touch with your brother's widow, Dillon thought, but he kept the comment to himself. ''First of all, it wasn't just *Keith's* house. It was Emily's, too, and she was perfectly within her rights to sell it. I'm sorry Mother is displeased, but, trust me, it was necessary.''

''Yes, well...she's especially furious that Emily is working for you,'' Charlotte went on. ''She refuses to believe that Keith died broke and in debt. According to her, if there truly is nothing left, then it had to be Emily who squandered the money, not Keith.''

Dillon gave a mirthless snort. ''Typical.''

''Yes, but there's more. She also says that if Emily is broke, then you owe it to your brother to support his widow, without her having to 'enslave herself to you.' Mother's words, not mine. I just thought you should know. The more she stews on the matter, the angrier she gets. By the time she comes home in the fall she will have worked up a full head of steam, so brace yourself.''

''Actually, I don't have a problem with supporting Emily, but she does. Trust me, if I offered she would refuse.''

''Good for her,'' Charlotte said emphatically. As a successful career woman, his sister had little sympathy for or patience with helpless females. For that matter, Adele herself was a tenured professor, but Dillon supposed she had to find some way to blame him for Emily's financial woes.

''However,'' his sister went on, ''that attitude is just going to annoy Mother.''

''Emily is probably used to that. She's not exactly

Mother's favorite person in the best of times, is she? She hasn't even bothered to call Emily but…what? Twice since she left Houston in January?''

''I know. I'm sorry, but you know how she is.''

''Yeah, I know. Look, sis, don't worry about it. I can handle Mother. Just do me a favor, and keep her there for as long as you can. Okay?''

Charlotte laughed. ''I'll do my best. But you're going to owe me big, little brother.''

When he hung up the telephone, Dillon left the tea to steep and went to the bedroom door and tapped softly. Getting no response, he peeked inside.

Emily lay on her side with her eyes closed. She looked exhausted. There were dark circles under her eyes and her face was pale as parchment.

He eased the door shut again and wandered into the living room. On edge, he paced the small space. He peered out the window, examined the books in the bookshelf, and one by one, picked up the knickknacks scattered around.

Finally he flopped down onto the sofa. With his head propped against the back cushion and his long legs stretched out in front of him he stared at the ceiling and willed his emotions to settle.

No matter how hard he tried he couldn't stop picturing the bewildered look on Emily's face when he asked why she hadn't told him about her morning sickness.

She hadn't a clue about how he felt. Not a clue.

How that grated.

Still…Dillon knew he ought to be glad. It was too soon. She wasn't ready. Hell, she might never be ready. He had to accept that. Especially once he told her the truth about the baby.

However, if he was going to have a chance with her at all he had to bide his time and let the past recede.

After the baby came and a little time had passed, he'd make his move.

Until then, he had to make sure she remained in the dark about his love for her. The best way to do that was go on as he'd been doing—keeping his distance whenever possible, and feigning indifference when it wasn't.

Dillon's eyes narrowed. Today had certainly proven one thing. Gert had been right about Emily attracting other men.

His confrontation with Grady had eliminated the competition from that quarter. For the time being, at least. After the baby was born it would be a different story.

A sound from the bedroom had him bolting off the sofa and sprinting through the apartment.

Bursting into the bedroom, he found Emily looking sickly green and staggering for the bathroom with one hand on her stomach and the other over her mouth. Horrified that he had caught her in her nightgown, she tried to wave him away, but he ignored her distress and swooped her up in his arms and rushed into the bathroom with her.

For the third time in just a few hours she once again emptied her stomach of its contents, while Dillon cupped her forehead in one hand and held her hair back with the other.

After a while, she was so weak and listless she seemed to stop caring that he was seeing her in her nightclothes or how humiliating the situation was or how awful she looked. After the terrible retching all she wanted was to rinse out her mouth, crawl back into bed and close her eyes.

However, Dillon wouldn't let her rest until she'd taken a few sips of tea and she'd nibbled on a cracker, neither of which she wanted.

Despite his efforts, she was sick three more times, and each time he played nursemaid, then carried her back to bed and coaxed more tea and crackers down her.

Around six, Eric stopped by and gave Dillon her car keys.

"Her car's in her assigned slot and locked. How's she doing?" he murmured in a hushed voice, peering around Dillon into the apartment.

"Not good. But at least she's resting now."

"Tough break, turning up pregnant after your husband is killed," he said quietly, revealing that word of Emily's condition had already spread among the construction crew. Grady hadn't wasted any time.

"My wife was sick as a dog with each one of our kids," Eric added. "Tea and crackers helped settled her stomach. If that didn't work, a cola over shaved ice would usually do the trick. Maybe Emily ought to try one of those."

Dillon's mouth twisted. "Thanks. I'll tell her."

After Eric left Dillon roamed the apartment, keeping an ear cocked for any sounds of distress from the bedroom, but there was only silence, and every time he peeked in on Emily she was sleeping peacefully.

By midnight, she hadn't been sick in almost seven hours and showed no sign of waking. Though he didn't feel comfortable leaving her, he knew she wouldn't want him to spend the night, so he left her a note, turned out the lights and let himself out of the apartment.

Emily awoke before dawn the next morning half expecting to find Dillon asleep on her living room sofa. When she discovered that he had gone she told herself that she was glad, and dismissed the little twinge in her chest as nothing more than the hollowness one feels after a spell of sickness.

In the kitchen she found the note he'd left. Emily's mouth compressed as she read the terse message in his neat, square handwriting, ordering her to stay home from work and get some rest. He'd even told her what she should eat for the next couple of days.

"Forget that," she muttered, tossing the note aside. She was starving.

"Who does he think he is, anyway?" she demanded of the walls.

Stomping around the kitchen, trying her best to work up some real anger, she filled the kettle with water and banged it down on the burner. She detested authoritative men, she told herself. Dillon had no business butting into her life and ordering her around. She certainly hadn't needed to be driven home. Nor had she needed him to stay with her.

She stomped to the refrigerator, intending to jerk it open, but at the last second she paused with her hand on the handle, a faraway look in her eyes.

Still...she *was* a little wobbly. In his own gruff way, Dillon had been thoughtful. How could you get angry with a man when he was just trying to look after you?

Actually, if she were completely honest with herself, she had to admit, it was kind of nice to have a man concern himself with her well-being. God knew, Keith had never put himself out for her in that way. At least, not to the extent that Dillon had.

Oh, her husband had showered her with expensive gifts, and he'd been charming and romantic when it suited him, but he never worried about whether or not she was happy or healthy or feeling well. He had never been particularly thoughtful or shown her any of the small, everyday kindnesses that caused love to deepen and grow—things like bringing her a cup of coffee in the mornings, or tossing an extra blanket over her on a cold winter's night, or calling home to check on her when he knew she wasn't feeling well.

Emily opened the refrigerator door and froze, her breath catching. Foolish tears filled her eyes as she stared at the bowl on the middle shelf. Nor had Keith ever made her Jell-O to pamper her abused tummy after an illness.

She pulled out the bowl and stared mistily at the shaky red gelatin. Even if Dillon had been thinking only of the baby, it had still been a sweet thing to do.

Taking a spoon from the drawer, she leaned back against the counter and ate right out of the bowl, her expression sadly meditative.

In the past she had made excuses for Keith, telling herself that he was simply not the solicitous type. Plus his work at the clinic kept him too busy to be attentive to her, and that it was natural for husbands to take their wives for granted.

Deep down, though, she'd known that it simply never occurred to Keith to put someone else before himself.

To give him his due, he had been an excellent oncologist, but it had been the disease that had interested

Keith, not the people that the dreadful malady had affected. To him, cancer was a fascinating puzzle, beating back its insidious spread a challenge that he relished.

Keith had perfected a charming bedside manner that had made his patients adore him, and he had reveled in their adulation because it fed his ego, but he hadn't truly empathized with them or cared about them as people.

Emily closed her eyes, her expression pained. It was a difficult admission to make about the man you had loved, the man with whom you'd shared your life for seven years, the man who had fathered your child, but there it was.

Such thoughts had been coming to her frequently over the last few months. She supposed that they'd been there all along and she'd simply kept them buried deep inside her because she hadn't wanted to face the truth about her husband or her marriage, but the hurtful circumstances surrounding Keith's death had set them free, she thought sadly.

She looked down at the quivering red gelatin and poked it with her spoon, a bemused smile curving her mouth. Who would have thought that a gruff, taciturn, rawly masculine man like Dillon would turn out to be the considerate one?

Chapter Nine

"You should ask Dillon. He'd be happy to do it."

"Oh, I don't think—"

"Ask me what?"

Gert and Emily looked up as the door opened and Dillon came striding in from outside, bringing with him a blast of hot, June air and the smell of sunshine. Stopping in front of Emily's desk, he took off his hard hat and cocked one eyebrow. "Well?"

Flustered, Emily squirmed under his intent stare. "Um, nothing. I-it's not important. Really. Forget it."

"Don't be silly, child." Ignoring Emily's frantic signal, Gert barreled on. "Emily is starting Lamaze classes and she asked me to be her coach. I'd be happy and honored to do it, but I'm already committed to a Bible study class two nights a week for the rest of the summer. At my age, that's about all I can handle. But I told her you could probably coach her."

"Gert, that's not—"

Dillon's intense gaze switched back to Emily. "Sure. No problem."

"No, really. It's too much to ask," she insisted in a near panic. Her opinion of him may have improved since she'd started working there, but that did not mean they had grown any closer.

Granted, their relationship had become one of odd extremes. Most of the time he seemed not to notice that she was around, yet whenever she needed help he was always there, Johnny on the spot, perfectly willing to perform even the most personal of tasks—like holding her head while she was sick and tucking her into bed wearing nothing more than a filmy nightgown.

Still...the very idea of Dillon performing such an intimate service as coaching her through childbirth made her heart flutter and sent scalding color racing to every square inch of her skin.

"I...I know how busy you are, Dillon. Anyway, you've done so much for me already, I couldn't ask you to do this, too."

"You don't have to ask. I'm volunteering. To tell you the truth, I'm happy for the chance. There's nothing I'd like more than to be in on your baby's birth."

He meant it, Emily realized in amazement, and she was both touched and panicked. How did you tell a man no after a statement like that?

"And so you should be," Gert declared. "You are the babe's uncle after all."

"I...I don't think you realize what you're volunteering for. You'd have to be there the entire time to coach me through the labor. And you'd be right there in the delivery room during the birth. That...that can be pretty intense."

"What's the matter? Worried that I might faint?" A hint of a smile tugged at Dillon's mouth. "I think I can handle it."

"See there! What'd I tell you?" Gert crowed. "So it's all settled."

Dazed, unable to think of another thing to discourage him, Emily slumped back in her chair. "I...I guess it is." Oh, dear Lord. Dillon was going to be her coach. How had this happened?

"Good," he replied. "Just tell me what night and when you want me to pick you up, and I'll be there."

Over the next three days Emily fretted and worried, but no matter how she wracked her brain she could not think of a graceful way out. By the time Dillon picked her up for the class on Thursday evening she was nearly sick with nerves.

On the drive to the community center where the classes were being held, neither spoke. Emily sat hugging the pillow she'd been instructed to bring, and peeked at him out of the corner of her eye.

This intense, remote man was going to get down on the floor with her, like the soon-to-be fathers in the class would be doing with their wives, and support her through the stages of labor and delivery? She closed her eyes and shivered.

For all the good she was going to get out of the class she might as well have dropped it. The whole point of Lamaze was to learn to relax and focus your attention away from the pain of labor and childbirth. No way could she do that with Dillon barking instructions and those piercing eyes glaring at her. With him touching her.

The clean scents of soap and shampoo and some sort of woodsy cologne drifted over to tickle Emily's nose, and she peeked at him again.

He had obviously showered and shaved just before picking her up. The five-o'clock shadow he always had by quitting time was gone and his black hair was still damp. He had ruthlessly brushed it back until every strand lay neatly against his head, but it wouldn't stay that way for long. Already it had begun to spring up and curl as it dried.

Emily ran her gaze over his strong profile, and her heart gave a peculiar little flutter. He really was a handsome male specimen, she admitted. In a rugged, rough-hewn sort of way. In the past she'd always compared him with Keith's refined sophistication, but she was beginning to realize that there was definitely something to be said for raw masculinity. Dillon was big, brooding and brawny…and all man.

She supposed she could understand why that Eileen person and all the other women who called Dillon at the office almost daily were so interested.

Turning her head, Emily looked out the passenger window, smote with the oddest mix of dread, gratitude and guilt.

Since she was being so honest she might as well admit that Dillon wasn't really so bad. In his blunt, sometimes heavy-handed way, he had actually been very good to her these past six months. That he had acted out of a sense of duty didn't change that. Even now, he was just trying to help.

The five other couples and the instructor were waiting when Emily and Dillon walked into the classroom.

"Ah, good, we're all here," the instructor said. Stepping forward, she extended her hand. "You must be Emily Maguire. I'm Carol Benson, the instructor." She turned to Dillon. "And you are…?"

"Dillon Maguire," he replied, shaking the woman's outstretched hand.

The instructor took a moment to introduce them to the others, then clapped her hands briskly. "Okay, couples. If you will form a semicircle and sit down, we'll get started."

Taking Emily's hand, Dillon assisted her into a sitting position on the floor and dropped down beside her, and the other couples did the same.

Bracing on one arm, Dillon leaned back and draped his other arm over his up-raised knee. The casual position stretched his tight jeans even tighter over powerful thighs. To her horror, Emily found her gaze drawn to his crotch.

She sucked in her breath and jerked her gaze away, but not quickly enough to stop the scalding heat that flooded her from her toes to her scalp. She felt as though she'd been doused in gasoline and set on fire. Even her earlobes burned and throbbed.

Left with no choice but to brazen it out, she stared straight ahead at Carol Benson, mortified to the marrow of her bones. Her heart pounded, and for several seconds she could not hear a word Carol said for the buzzing in her ears. Had Dillon noticed?

Oh, please, oh, please, oh, please, don't let it be so, she silently entreated, keeping her eyes straight ahead. She didn't dare look at him. She didn't have the nerve.

What in heaven's name was the matter with her? Ogling a man like that. Particularly *this* man.

Emily drew several slow, deep breaths, willing her nerves to settle and squashing the fluttery wings of panic that beat inside her chest. It was perfectly natural, she assured herself. After all, she had been alone for over six months. Sexual deprivation. That was all it was. That, and of course her nerves were frazzled by having Dillon coach her. There was nothing to beat herself up about.

"All right, class. Now we're going to be practicing a few simple stretching exercises. These are designed to help the expectant mothers relax and foster a sense of partnership between the mothers and their coaches."

Emily sighed. Oh yeah, that was going to happen. She felt about as relaxed as a wound violin string.

Resigned, she did as she was told and lay back on her pillow while Dillon knelt at her feet. Though Emily heard Carol's instructions and knew what to expect, the feel of his large, callused hands closing around her ankles was so shocking she gasped and jerked as though she'd been poked with a cattle prod.

"What is it? Did I hurt you?" Dillon demanded, snatching his hands away and shooting her a worried look.

"No! No, not you. I, uh...it was just a little muscle spasm in my leg, that's all."

When he was satisfied that she was all right he took hold of her ankles again, then turned his attention back to Carol and listened intently to every word she spoke. Concentrating so fiercely his face looked like a thundercloud, Dillon began to manipulate Emily's legs and guide her through the exercises.

To her amazement, everything went smoothly. On reflection, Emily realized she should not have been surprised. Whatever Dillon undertook he gave it his all and did a thorough job of it, and this was no different.

Though he put her through her paces with utmost care, his strength ensured that she got a full workout. By the time they had finished the warmup, she was feeling pleasantly limp.

Next Carol explained the different stages of labor and demonstrated the proper breathing technique for each and had the women practicing them.

"Okay, class," she announced when they'd finished. "Now the men are going to practice timing labor. For this part you ladies just lie there and rest and let the men do the work.

"Now, coaches, your job is to reassure the mother-to-be and to direct and assist her. To do that you will have to monitor the contractions and begin breathing instructions the instant one starts. I'll demonstrate what I mean with this couple," she said, moving closer to Emily and Dillon.

"Mr. Maguire, I want you to move around to one side. That's it. Now, put your hand on your wife's tummy."

"What?" Emily's head came up off the pillow. "Oh. No, he's not my— Ow!" She winced and shot Dillon an accusing look when he gave her hand a hard squeeze, but he ignored her and smiled at the instructor.

"Do I press, or what?" he asked.

"No, just gently lay your palm on her, that's all."

Dillon's gaze zeroed in on the distended mound beneath Emily's blue maternity top.

His nostrils flared slightly as he drew in a bracing breath. He rubbed his palms on the legs of his jeans, then slowly reached out with his right hand. It hovered, not quite steady, the long, callused fingers spread. Then, as gentle as thistledown, his hand settled onto Emily's tummy.

She caught her breath. Tanned by hours in the sun, his skin was a deep bronze against the powder-blue maternity top and so large it practically covered her abdomen. Dillon's gaze met hers for a second, but as though unable to resist, he looked back at the mound beneath his hand.

Emily closed her eyes and lay rigid as stone. She could barely breathe. Even through her maternity top the imprint of his hand seared her flesh like a branding iron. She could feel each individual finger, the broad palm, the incredible warmth.

Dear Lord, she groaned silently. He was just touching her lightly. There was nothing sexual or provocative about it. Nevertheless, she'd never experienced anything so intimate in her life.

Opening her eyes a slit, she studied Dillon's hard profile through the veil of her lashes. He stared at her abdomen, his face set in its usually unreadable mask. What was he thinking? What emotions did he feel? If any.

"If your mother-to-be was actually in labor, as the contraction started you would feel a definite tightening of the abdominal muscles," Carol went on. "Coaches, that will be your cue to begin urging her to perform stage one breathing. Also, be sure to immediately check your watches so that you can time both the duration of each contraction and the interval between them. And remember, coaches, keep your voices soft. You're giving encouragement, not issuing orders."

Through the first "pretend" contraction Dillon dutifully kept his hand on Emily's tummy and his gaze glued to his wristwatch. During the lull afterwards he followed Carol's instructions to the letter, massaging Emily's shoulders, periodically dabbing her "perspiring" face and murmuring words of praise.

Carol signaled another contraction, and he moved back to Emily's side. He had barely placed his hand on her tummy again when the baby gave a tremendous kick.

"Whoa!" Dillon jerked his hand back as though he'd accidentally touched a high-voltage wire. His head whipped around, and his gaze locked with Emily's.

"Didn't that hurt?" he demanded.

She shook her head, both amused by his shocked expression and embarrassed at the incredible intimacy they had just shared.

"Not at all?"

"No, it just feels kind of strange. And wonderful," she added with a self-conscious smile.

He shook his head. "Amazing."

He stared at her abdomen for several seconds, then reached out and carefully laid his hand on her stomach again. As though responding to his touch, the baby kicked vigorously for several seconds. Dillon's eyes widened. "Wow."

His gaze sought hers again, and Emily's heart swelled with so much emotion her chest was a massive ache. Gone was the usual granite-hard set to his face. In its place was an expression she had never thought to see there—one of utter joy and awe.

* * *

Emily detested filing almost as much as Gert did. She had been at the dreaded chore for almost an hour when Dillon came barreling out of his office.

"If anybody needs me, I'll be at the east end of the site with Eric," he announced in his usual terse tone.

At the door, he reached for the knob, then stopped as though something had just occurred to him and looked at Emily with a distracted frown creasing his brow. "This shouldn't take long, but if I'm not back by quitting time, just page me."

"You don't have to hurry back on my account. I don't mind waiting," Emily assured him.

His gaze flickered over her burgeoning tummy, and he shook his head. "No, you need to go home and put your feet up. So page me when you're ready to leave."

Without giving her a chance to respond, he crammed his hard hat on his head, jerked the door open and took off.

"What was that all about?" Gert asked, arching one eyebrow at Emily.

"Nothing really. I, uh...had a little trouble with my car, so Dillon gave me a ride to work this morning."

"I see. Well, that's good."

"Yes. It's very nice of him," Emily agreed in a small voice, stuffing a purchase order into a file.

A brief silence followed, but she felt Gert studying her.

"So how are the Lamaze classes going?"

Emily's heart skipped a beat. "Oh, fine."

"Hmm. So, Dillon is turning out to be an acceptable coach, after all, is he?"

"Yes."

"Good. I'm glad. And you two are getting along okay?" Gert persisted.

Glancing over her shoulder, Emily sent her what she hoped was a reassuring smile. "Yes. We get along fine."

She paused in the act of searching for a file, her gaze drifting out the window to follow Dillon, striding away toward the construction site. It was the truth, she supposed, although fine was an inadequate word to describe the interaction between her and Dillon these days.

She had come to work at Maguire Construction determined to keep her distance and maintain their cool relationship but that had proved impossible.

Emily's mouth took on a wry twist. It was difficult to remain aloof from a man when he was rubbing your back and tummy and being so solicitous.

Somehow, in the five weeks since he'd appointed himself her Lamaze coach, before she'd quite realized what was happening, she and Dillon had become friends.

No matter how much she protested, he insisted on looking after her.

Emily glanced guiltily at Gert. Dillon hadn't driven her to work that morning because of mechanical trouble with her car, as Emily had led the older woman to believe. The problem was that recently she had gotten so large it made driving difficult. Actually, darn near impossible, and certainly dangerous, for her and every other poor hapless soul on the road with her. When she had jokingly mentioned that to Dillon he had not only started giving her a ride to and from work, he had started chauffeuring her everywhere.

He'd taken her shopping for baby equipment at the mall and put together the crib and changing table she'd bought. He ran errands for her, drove her to and from work, to the grocery store, the pharmacy, the dry cleaners, and the beauty parlor and anywhere else she wanted or needed to go. He'd even started taking her to her appointments with Dr. Conn.

Actually, looking back, Emily realized that their relationship had begun to change even before the Lamaze classes, though that had certainly hastened the process.

At first the change had been nothing more than a subtle shift in her perception of him on closer acquaintance. From there, day-to-day association with Dillon had begun to chip away at her long-held opinion about the kind of man he was.

There were probably other factors, as well. Maybe finally facing the whole truth about Keith had allowed her to think more objectively, she mused. Or maybe she'd just finally been able to see past Dillon's gruff exterior. Thinking back to the day he had taken care of her when she'd been sick, Emily smiled. Or perhaps the real catalyst for change had been something as simple as a bowl of red gelatin left in her refrigerator.

Whatever the reason, somewhere along the way she began to see him in a different light—not as an adversary, or an annoyance, or even a brother-in-law, but as a man. A caring, thoughtful, dependable man.

Of course, not everything had changed. Dillon still made her uncomfortable and edgy, and his raw masculinity still overwhelmed her, but at least she no longer had the urge to turn and flee whenever he was near. Nor did the mere sight of him rub her the wrong way.

On the contrary, it wasn't Emily's temper that Dillon ignited these days, but something else altogether. To her horror and chagrin, since he had become her Lamaze coach she found herself, not merely conscious of him as a man, but actually attracted to him physically.

Emily blamed it on her pregnancy. She had read that in the last trimester some women experienced heightened sexual desire. She supposed, when you considered that she'd been alone for seven months, it wasn't so surprising that her hormones were running amok, but of all the men in the world, why did it have to be Dillon who got her all hot and bothered?

She had only to catch sight of him moving through the construction site or huddled in a discussion with a group of workers, for her brain to short-circuit and her libido to take over. One glimpse and she stopped whatever she was doing and stared like a besotted teenager. As she was doing at that very moment, she realized.

Annoyed with herself, she jerked her gaze away from Dillon's receding form, crammed the last folder into the cabinet and slammed the drawer shut.

"Something wrong?" Gert asked, looking up from her work as Emily waddled back to her desk.

"No. I just hate filing, that's all."

"Humph. Can't say as I blame you," the other woman muttered, and went back to entering data on the computer.

Emily sat down at her desk and picked up the pile of invoices that had accumulated since that morning and started sorting them. That she was experiencing this inappropriate attraction was awful enough, but even more humiliating, it was completely one-sided.

Granted, Dillon seemed more relaxed around her now, and certainly he was more pleasant and friendly. They were more at ease with each other and talked more comfortably together, and occasionally he even laughed with her.

As her pregnancy progressed and she grew bigger and bigger he seemed mesmerized by the changes in her body. In his gruff way he showered her with all the attention and caring that any woman could hope for, even from a husband—attention she knew in her heart that she would not have received from Keith.

However, that was as far as he went. Never, not once, not by so much as a look, did he give any indication that he was interested in her as anything but a friend.

And that made her feel like a complete idiot.

Emily sighed. Ah, well. No matter how much she chastised herself, it did not help. There was just something so earthy and appealing about Dillon—whether he wore his usual heavy work boots, jeans and casual shirt or a designer suit—that she could not ignore.

In his work clothes he was the epitome of rugged masculine appeal—six foot four inches of lean-hipped, broad-shouldered brawn and brains that never failed to make her insides flutter. On those days when he came directly from the main office looking as though he'd just stepped out of *GQ,* his impact was equally lethal.

Realizing where her thoughts had once again strayed, Emily groaned softly and ground her teeth. Dear Lord, she was hopeless.

* * *

He was pathetic, Dillon thought. A pathetic coward. He should tell Emily the truth—now, before the baby arrived. It was the right thing to do. The honorable thing.

Deep in thought, he headed back to the office, his long stride eating up the ground. On his way he passed a number of his crew, jovially calling out farewells and bawdy jeers to one another as they headed for their cars. It was Friday, payday and quitting time, and they were looking forward to the weekend. Eric and a few others called out to Dillon, as well, but the somber look on his face made them do a double take and give him a wide berth.

Dillon was so preoccupied he didn't notice.

The trouble was, after all these years, Emily was finally beginning to trust him, even to like him a little. These past weeks, spending so much time in each other's company, doing ordinary, everyday things together, had been wonderful. He sure as hell didn't want to ruin that, especially not now, when they were developing a tentative friendship of sorts.

''Yeah, but the trouble is, you're cultivating that friendship under false pretenses,'' he muttered to himself. ''And you might as well face it, Maguire, the guilt is eating you alive.''

He had to set the record straight. He knew that. It was only right. Emily deserved to know the truth. But damn, how he dreaded doing it.

Dillon spat out a shocking curse and aimed a vicious kick at a crushed soft drink can that someone had tossed on the ground, sending it sailing.

All right, dammit. He'd tell her tonight, he vowed as he neared the office trailer. He'd take her out to dinner. Afterwards, when she was feeling relaxed and mellow, he'd tell her.

She was going to be upset. He had no doubt about that. Upset, hell. She'd probably hate him. And who could blame her. He'd helped Keith deceive her. Then he'd lied to her by keeping quiet about the deception. That made him just as guilty.

Dillon ground his teeth. So be it. If he had to go back to square one with her, then that's what he'd do. But one way or another, even if it took another seven years, he would eventually make things right between them somehow.

Outside the office he paused and drew a deep breath, then, his face set with grim determination, he jerked open the door and stepped inside.

Emily looked up and smiled. "You're back. And right on time, too."

"Yeah. You ready?"

"Just a sec." She cleared her desk and covered her computer, then got her purse out of the bottom drawer and stood. "All set. Good night, Gert. Have a nice weekend," she called.

Skirting around the corner of her desk, she started toward the door, but after only two waddling steps she came to a halt, a look of astonishment on her face. "Oh, my. I think…I'm…"

"Emily!" Dillon barked, as she crumpled to the floor.

He leaped forward, his heart in his throat. "Emily! Oh, God, Emily," he gasped, dropping down beside her.

"Oh, my Lord, that poor child."

Gert came hurrying over, wringing her hands, but Dillon paid no attention to her. He brushed Emily's hair off her face and patted her cheek smartly. "Emily. Emily, wake up. Talk to me."

She looked so pale and lifeless Dillon's terror ratcheted up several notches, making his chest so tight he could barely breathe. Frantic, he chafed one of her wrists, then the other, but she still did not respond.

"Should I call an ambulance?" Gert fretted.

"No, that'll take too long." In one motion Dillon swooped Emily up in his arms, bounded to his feet and strode for the door. "I'm taking her to St. John's Hospital. Call Dr. Conn at the clinic and tell him to meet us in the E.R."

"What? That's impossible." Emily stared at Dr. Conn, appalled.

"Emily, you're threatening to miscarry. If you want to save this baby, you must stay in bed for the remainder of your pregnancy."

"But—"

"Look, I know it seems like a terrible ordeal to go through, but it won't be for that long—six or seven weeks, that's all."

"You don't understand. It's not that. I can't quit my job. It's my only means of support."

"You don't have a choice."

"That's right. You don't."

At the flat pronouncement, both Emily and Dr. Conn turned their heads and looked at Dillon.

He stood leaning against the wall of the small emergency room cubicle, his arms folded over his chest, his face like a black cloud. His was the first face Emily had seen when she regained consciousness.

The nurses and doctors who had been on duty when

he'd carried her into the E.R. over an hour ago had tried to get him to wait outside, quoting hospital policy, but he had told them in explicit and colorful terms exactly what they could do with their rules and planted himself where he was now standing. Since then no one had again dared to try and make him leave.

"If the doctor says you should stay in bed, then that's where you'll stay," Dillon stated in an implacable tone. "And forget about your job. As of this moment, you no longer work for Maguire Construction."

"Dillon! You know I can't afford—"

"Don't worry about the money. That won't be a problem because I'm taking you home with me."

"What! I can't live with you!"

"Well, you certainly can't live alone in that tiny apartment. You'll need someone to look after you and help you twenty-four hours a day. Even if I hired a live-in nurse there isn't room at your place for another person."

"I don't need a nurse. I can't afford one."

"Yeah, well, I can. And I'm hiring one. So for once you're just going to have to swallow that stiff-necked pride of yours."

"For the record, I think Dillon has an excellent idea." Dr. Conn stuck his stethoscope into the pocket of his lab coat and moved toward the exit. "However, I'm going to let you two hash this over in private. Just remember, Emily, no matter where you live, for the next six weeks you are to stay off your feet. Period."

The instant the doctor disappeared through the curtain Emily turned to Dillon and snapped, "I mean it, Dillon. I can't move in with you."

"Why not?"

"I just can't, that's all." Unable to meet his demanding stare, she lowered her gaze and studied her fingers as they plucked nervously at the sheet covering her.

Out of the corner of her eye she saw Dillon cock his head to one side and narrow his eyes. "Ah hell, you're worried about appearances, aren't you? Just like when you kicked me out after Keith died."

"So what if I am," she said in a defensive tone.

"Dammit, Emily, what's the big deal? These days unmarried couples live together all the time. Some aren't even romantically involved. They're just roommates, for Pete's sake."

"That may be, but I spent my formative years with elderly grandparents. Maybe the values and morals they instilled in me are out of date, but they're part of who I am. No matter how times may have changed, I just wouldn't feel comfortable living with you."

"I see." Dillon studied her with unnerving directness for so long she had to fight the urge to squirm. Finally, he nodded.

"All right then. If you won't move in with me and let me take care of you, then there's only one thing left to do. As soon as I can arrange it, we'll get married."

Chapter Ten

"*Married?*" Emily gaped at Dillon. "You and me? You can't be serious."

"Do you have a better idea? You won't let me support you. You won't move in with me. Marriage is the only other choice you have, unless you're willing to go on welfare. Somehow, I don't think you want that."

"No. Of course not. But this isn't fair to you. You're a confirmed bachelor. Keith always said you weren't the marrying kind, that you liked playing the field. I know the last thing you want is to get married."

Dillon stared at her, his expression inscrutable. "No offense, Emily, but you don't have any idea *what* I want."

"Maybe not," she conceded, oddly hurt by his

harsh tone. "But marriage is a huge step. Why on earth would you even consider it?"

"So that you and the baby can get through this safely," he replied in a voice devoid of emotion. "That child is my flesh and blood, remember. I'll do whatever is necessary to protect you both."

"I see." She lowered her gaze again to her plucking fingers and told herself it was foolish to feel hurt. What had she expected? A declaration of undying love? "What, uh…what happens after the baby is born?"

"The same thing that usually happens. We'll raise the child together. The three of us will be a family."

"Then, you, uh…you intend for this to be a real marriage?" Emily felt her face flame. She had barely managed to get the words out, but she had to know.

Dillon fixed her with another of his intense stares. He was silent so long a little prickle danced down her spine. "Yes," he replied finally. "In every way. But not until you're ready."

"But that's not fair to you either. What if you meet someone else and fall in love?"

"Trust me. That's not going to happen."

"You can't be sure of that."

"I'm sure. Look, you'll just have to take my word for it. Believe me, that won't be a problem. Unlike my brother, I take marriage very seriously. I swear to you, Emily, I'll never be unfaithful. When I make a commitment, it's forever."

Emily's heart pounded. She gazed into that hard face, those vivid eyes and knew with absolute certainty that he was telling the truth. For all his gruffness and slightly rough-around-the-edges manner, Dillon possessed many fine qualities that Keith, with his abundance of charm and personality and expensive Ivy-League education, had not.

Dillon was a man of bedrock-solid values, a man of integrity, honest and loyal and utterly reliable. A man to whom a woman could entrust her heart and know that he would treat it with the utmost care and tenderness. Furthermore, if she was ever lucky enough to win his love, it would be hers forever.

Nor did it hurt that he was handsome and sexy. It embarrassed her to admit it, particularly given her condition, but he appealed to her on a physical level more than any man she'd ever known. Including Keith.

The admission brought with it a little dart of surprise, but there was no denying it. Funny, she had known Dillon for over seven years and yet she'd only just recently become aware of him in that way.

Probably she'd blocked out the attraction out of loyalty to Keith, and all those years she'd kept it at bay by erecting a wall of cool animosity between them.

Now, however, the mere idea of making love with Dillon made her feel flushed and jittery.

"Then you'd...you'd be content with a loveless marriage?"

"I didn't say that. In the days of arranged marriages couples often grew to care deeply for one another. I think you and I have a shot at that. These past weeks we've managed to rub along together well enough, haven't we?"

"Well, yes. I suppose so."

"I think we've also discovered recently that we like many of the same things. And that we have the same values."

Emily wrinkled her nose at that, and a ghost of a smile tugged at Dillon's mouth. "Okay, so my attitude about co-habitation is a little more liberal than yours," he conceded. "But *most* of the time our values mesh. My point is, these past months we've knocked down some old barriers and become friends. Well...sort of, anyway. Haven't we?"

At her nod, a look of satisfaction came over his face. "Well, then, I'm sure we can build on that."

"But, Dillon, even if all you say is true, it's too soon. Keith—"

"I know, I know. It's only been a little over seven months since you lost him. Since we lost him. But this is an unusual situation. Given the circumstances I think we can set aside convention. I think Keith would even approve."

Emily smiled wanly. She seriously doubted that. For all his catting around, Keith had thought of her as his and his alone. He would hate the idea of her marrying again. Particularly of her marrying Dillon.

Though, in his own way, Keith had loved his older brother, just beneath the surface of that emotion had existed an undercurrent of rivalry and competition, even jealousy, on his part that Emily had never understood. True, Dillon had built a successful business on his own and in the process had amassed a fortune, but Keith had been equally successful in his field. Maybe not monetarily, but in other ways. Keith's attitude just hadn't made sense to her.

Unfolding his arms, Dillon pushed away from the wall and moved to stand beside the gurney on which Emily lay. He picked up her hand and studied it as he massaged the silky skin and delicate bones. After a moment he looked up, his gaze locking with hers. "Well? What do you say?"

Wracked with indecision, Emily caught her lower lip between her teeth and gazed at him, torn. Her chest was so tight she could barely breathe. As little as a few months ago she would have been appalled at the very idea of marrying Dillon and would have refused without the least hesitation. Now, though common sense and propriety dictated otherwise, it wasn't that easy.

Oh, he was persuasive, she thought. It was a crazy idea. She shouldn't even be considering it. She had not been a widow that long, and she wasn't in love with Dillon. Of course she wasn't.

There were probably at least a dozen other valid reasons why she should say no as well. She just couldn't think of them right now.

So why don't you just thank him politely and refuse?

Emily closed her eyes and silently groaned. Because, heaven help her, she didn't want to. Foolish and reckless as it undoubtedly was, the mere thought of being married to Dillon was thrilling and irresistible.

Come to that, she could do worse, she told herself. Despite his gruff exterior, she knew that Dillon would be a wonderful husband and father.

And an exciting lover.

She drew in a deep breath and came to a decision. Before she could change her mind she opened her eyes and looked at him. "All right. I'll marry you."

His only detectable reaction was a slight flaring of his nostrils. For the briefest instant Emily thought she saw something flash in his eyes—something joyful and exultant—but it was gone before she could be certain. Or maybe it had been nothing more than wishful thinking on her part. His expression had not changed one iota, not by so much as a twitch of a muscle.

"Good. I'm glad that's settled."

Disappointment fluttered through Emily, but she quickly squashed it. What did you expect? That he would scoop you up in his arms and twirl you around, delirious with joy? It's not as though marriage was something he desired. The man was doing the noble thing and giving up his single lifestyle out of a strong sense of family responsibility.

The bare truth was, they were both going into this for the sake of the baby. *And you'd do well to remember that,* she sternly reminded herself.

Actually, it was probably best this way, she told herself. When she'd married Keith she'd been starry-eyed and blinded by love, and look what that had gotten her.

She folded her hands together on top of the sheet and gave him a tentative smile. "So…what now?"

"Now I'll make the arrangements. If all goes well, we can have the ceremony the first of next week."

"That soon? But what if Adele can't make it back by then?"

"It won't matter. I have no intention of telling her until it's a done deal."

"Dillon! She's your mother! We *have* to invite her to the wedding." Emily grimaced. "Lord knows, she's going to be upset enough with me for not telling her about the baby before this, and I suppose I deserve that, but if we don't at least tell her we're getting married she's going to be livid. She'll never forgive either of us.''

He gave a bark of mirthless laughter. ''So what else is new?''

He studied her worried expression and shook his head. ''You really don't get it, do you, Emily? It wouldn't matter if we gave her six months notice, she's not going to approve of this marriage. In fact, if she knew what we were planning she'd do everything in her power to stop us. So why put ourselves through that?''

Emily continued to argue, but her attempts were halfhearted at best, and in the end Dillon prevailed. Deep down, she knew that he was right. Adele had never liked her. Nevertheless Emily had no doubt that she would disapprove of her marrying again so soon after Keith's death. Though it was cowardly and made her feel guilty, she was secretly relieved that she would not have to deal with her mother-in-law just yet.

''Besides, Dr. Conn's instructions were very clear,'' Dillon insisted. ''You're to stay calm and avoid any sort of stress or upset.''

''I guess you're right,'' she conceded. ''Though you do realize, there's going to be hell to pay when your mother does find out.''

''We'll face that when it happens. I'll have your telephone number switched to a second line at my place. That way, if Charlotte or Mother call you they'll think they've reached you at your apartment.''

''Isn't that kind of devious?''

''Sure, but if it saves you from being subjected to one of Mother's frenzied furies during the next six weeks, it'll be worth it.'' He smiled crookedly and gave her chin a mock cuff. "With any luck, by the time she returns and learns the truth the baby will be here and you'll be back in fighting form."

"A lot of good that will do. Your mother and I aren't exactly evenly matched," Emily replied morosely. Far from it. In a full-blown rage, Adele Maguire was hell on wheels.

Dillon instantly sobered. "Hey, I was just kidding. Don't worry about it. I won't let her unload on you. When the time comes, I'll deal with her myself."

The following Monday, Emily was released from the hospital. That evening, with her lying propped up on the sofa in the living room of Dillon's penthouse apartment and him standing beside her, looking breathtakingly handsome in a charcoal suit, white shirt and silvery gray tie, they were married.

Mercifully, the only guests were Gert, Eric and his wife, Dr. Conn, and Mrs. Taggert, Dillon's housekeeper. Even though everyone present knew her history, Emily was nevertheless self-conscious about getting married when she was so obviously pregnant.

She was almost sick with nerves and went through the ceremony in a daze, barely aware of the minister's words or exchanging vows with Dillon. When he slipped a diamond-encrusted band on her wedding finger she caught her breath and stared at the sparkling ring in shock. It must have cost a fortune.

Before she knew it, the ceremony was over and, beaming at them, the minister pronounced, "You may now kiss your bride."

Jolted out of her stupor, Emily's eyes widened when Dillon sat down on the edge of the sofa facing her. Staring into his vivid blue eyes, she read the intent there, and her heart began to hammer against her rib cage.

His hard mouth curved into the faintest of smiles as he reached out and gathered her into his arms. "Relax," he advised in a teasing murmur. "This won't hurt a bit. I promise."

Lazily, his gaze trailed down her face. For the space of several heartbeats he stared at her lips, parted in surprise, and slowly, as though weighted with lead, his eyelids began to droop and his head tipped to one side.

Emily felt his breath feather across her face and excitement pounded through her. She could barely draw breath. Unconsciously, the tip of her tongue peeked out and swept over her suddenly dry lips. Through slitted lids fringed with sweeping black lashes, Dillon's eyes glittered like blue diamonds.

Then he pulled her close, gathered her against his chest with both arms and pressed his lips to hers.

The kiss was stunning—soft as summer rain, yet it carried the punch of a lightning bolt. At the first shocking touch of his lips on hers, Emily's heart lurched to a halt, then took off at a gallop.

His mouth rocked against hers, warm and masterful, yet at the same time exquisitely tender. Emily's head began to spin and her pulse thrummed, but before she could react the brief caress ended.

Raising his head, Dillon looked into her dazed eyes and smiled. "Hello, wife," he whispered.

"He-hello," Emily whispered back.

Their gazes locked in silent exchange, and for several seconds it was as though they were the only two people in the room. Soon though they became aware of the laughter and clapping all around them. With a rueful smile, Dillon eased her back onto the mound of pillows and stood to accept their friends' congratulations and best wishes.

While the women crowded around Emily to kiss her cheek and admire her ring, Dillon shook hands with the men and tolerated their teasing comments and slaps on the back with good grace.

Despite the short notice, there was a small buffet spread and cake, courtesy of Gert and Mrs. Taggert.

For the next hour, while everyone ate and milled around and talked, Emily grappled with nerves and conflicting emotions.

On the one hand, she wished that everyone would leave, and on the other, the thought of being alone with Dillon made her so jittery she felt as though a thousand butterflies had taken up residence in her stomach.

"Is something wrong?"

Starting guiltily, Emily looked up as Dillon hitched one hip onto the sofa back and leaned over her. She wrinkled her nose at him and shrugged. "Not really."

"Then why the glum face?"

"It's just that I feel so...so conspicuous."

"Why? Everyone here is a friend. And they're all aware of the situation."

"I know, but...well...getting married when I'm seven and a half months pregnant just feels weird, that's all. Especially lying here propped up like this."

Emily just couldn't help herself. Not only was she nervous, she also had a bad case of the "poor me's." Angling a pouty look at Dillon from beneath her lashes, she plucked at the new blue silk and lace maternity dress that he had miraculously produced for the occasion. "Brides are supposed to be radiant and beautiful, but I just feel like a big ole beached whale."

Dillon's reaction was not at all what she expected. He threw his head back and burst out laughing.

The rich, full-bodied masculine guffaws rumbled up from deep inside him and drew the attention of everyone in the room.

The deep baritone sounds shocked Emily and sent a tingle racing over her skin. His delighted mirth totally transformed his stern face. Against his tanned skin his teeth flashed a startling white and his eyes twinkled with good humor, the skin at their corners crinkling attractively.

Thunderstruck, Emily stared at him. Somber, Dillon was an attractive man, but laughing he was so handsome he took her breath away. The transformation was so amazing she wondered why he didn't laugh more often.

"A *whale!*" he finally managed to choke out. "Oh, sweetheart, you're priceless. You really are." Subduing the last of his chuckles, Dillon wiped at his moist eyes and grinned at her. Then his expression softened to tenderness as he reached out and stroked her jaw with his forefinger. "Trust me. You look like a glowing Madonna—so beautiful."

Shocked speechless, all Emily could do was gape at him, while her heart knocked against her ribs and excitement zinged through her like a high-voltage current of electricity. Finally she unstuck her tongue from the roof of her mouth and stammered, "You...you think I'm beautiful?"

The question was barely out when she saw the distant expression he usually wore slip back over his face and felt him almost imperceptibly pull back from her emotionally.

He shrugged. "Sure. I always have. I'd have to be blind not to have noticed that."

Emily stared at him, but before she could gather her wits he stood. "Excuse me for a minute. I need to talk to Eric about a problem at the site." He walked away to join his foreman on the other side of the room, leaving her staring after him, thoroughly befuddled.

On reflection over the next half hour Emily decided that Dillon had simply been being nice in an effort to cajole her out of her self-conscious funk. After all, the man had ignored her and done his best to shut her out for years. She couldn't believe that he'd bothered to form an opinion about her looks, one way or the other.

Suddenly Emily realized that while she had been puzzling over Dillon's comment Mrs. Taggert and Gert had cleared away the food and the mess and now everyone was preparing to leave. Once again her nerves began to twang at the prospect of being left alone with Dillon.

"Now, young woman, you stay in bed like I ordered and let Dillon pamper you, you hear?" Dr. Conn admonished as he patted her hand in farewell.

"I will," she replied with a nervous smile.

Eric and his wife repeated their well wishes, as did Mrs. Taggert. Then it was Gert's turn.

She sat down beside Emily on the sofa and gathered her into a motherly hug. "I hope you know how lucky you are," she whispered in Emily's ear. "He's a good man, Emily. Better than you know. And God knows, he's been eating his heart out long enough. Give him a chance. I promise you won't regret it."

The cryptic comment surprised Emily, momentarily distracting her, but Gert gave her no opportunity to ask what she meant. Getting to her feet, she turned to the others and made a shooing motion. "All right, everyone out. The party's over. Time to leave the newlyweds alone. Let's go," she ordered.

Amid pretend grumbling, everyone called out their best wishes to her while being herded toward the door. Emily laughed, but inside she was quaking. Dear Lord, what had she done? She was Mrs. Dillon Maguire.

All too soon everyone was gone and Dillon returned from the foyer.

He stopped in the arched doorway and looked at her, a faint smile curving his mouth. "Well, we did it."

Emily nervously twisted one corner of the afghan covering her legs. "Yes. Yes, we did."

He tipped his head to one side and studied her. "Are you okay? You look a little peaked."

"I'm fine."

"Maybe so," he said, though his expression said he didn't believe her. "But it's time you were in bed. It's been a hectic day."

"Oh, but—"

Ignoring her protest, he crossed to the sofa, swooped her up in his arms and strode out of the room and down the hall.

"Dillon, you don't have to carry me. Dr. Conn said I could get up to shower and use the bathroom so surely I can walk this far. I must weigh a ton."

"I don't think so. The doc was very specific about

what you could and could not do.'' He looked at her out of the corner of his eye and smiled crookedly. ''And just so you know, you're about as heavy as a feather pillow. I've lifted with one hand bags of cement that weigh more than you.''

Emily arched one eyebrow. ''Are you comparing me to a bag of cement?''

''Hardly.''

He carried her into the bedroom in which Gert had earlier unpacked her clothes and helped her get dressed for the ceremony and deposited her on the king-size bed. Someone—Mrs. Taggert, Emily assumed—had turned down the covers and laid out her teal nightgown.

''Do you need help getting undressed?''

''What? No!'' Emily shot him a horrified look and before she could stop herself she clamped both hands over her chest, as though she feared he would rip the lacy blue dress right off her. Instantly, she felt foolish, and in response her entire body suffused with heat. Mercifully, Dillon appeared not to notice. ''No, uh…thank you. I can manage.''

''Okay, if you're sure. Just toss your clothes on that chair over there and I'll hang them up later.'' He turned and headed out the door. ''And I'm warning you, don't dawdle in the bathroom too long or I'll come in and get you.''

''I won't.'' She started to wish him good-night, but he was already gone. Emily stared after him, feeling oddly disappointed.

This was their wedding night. True, it wasn't a love match, and she was big as a blimp, which no doubt was a huge turnoff to a man like Dillon who was accustomed to dating beautiful, sexy women. Intimacy was out of the question, of course, but still, he could have at least told her good-night.

Maybe even kissed her again, as he had after the ceremony.

Heaving a sigh, Emily stripped off her pretty new dress and shed her bra and panty hose, replacing them with the silky nightgown. Then, with utmost care and a great deal of struggle, she finally managed to climb to her feet and waddle to the bathroom.

Fifteen minutes later, her nighttime ritual done, she opened the door and jumped. "Dillon! What are you doing here?"

He waited just outside the door with his arms crossed over his chest, one shoulder propped casually against the wall. Her gaze flickered over him, and she experienced a rush of awareness so intense it sent little prickles skipping over her skin.

Barefoot, and smelling of toothpaste and virile male, he appeared to be wearing only a short robe. The lapels of the thigh-length garment gaped to the loosely knotted tie belt at his waist, revealing a brawny, bare chest covered with a mat of dark curls. Below the white terrycloth his legs were bare as well, long and muscular, the tanned skin liberally dusted with more dark hair.

"Waiting for you," he replied.

Emily let out a little squeak when, without warning, he swooped her up in his arms. "Dillon, really! You don't have to do this. I can walk to the bed."

"You heard the doc. You're to spend as little time on your feet as possible."

He crossed the room and deposited her on the bed. Emily smiled and lay back on the pillow as he pulled the covers up over her, tucking her in as though she were a child. Being fussed over and coddled was a new experience for her, and she had to admit, it was nice. His concern for her well-being made her feel warm inside.

Smiling contentedly, she snuggled deeper into the mattress and watched Dillon hang her dress on a padded hanger and disappear into the walk-in closet with it. When he emerged she opened her mouth to tell him good-night, only to suck in a sharp breath and stare as Dillon shrugged out of his robe and dropped it on a chair.

Eyes wide, Emily clutched the covers against her chest with both hands and stared at him. He wasn't completely naked beneath the robe, as she had thought, although the skimpy navy blue briefs did little to protect his modesty. "Wh-what are you doing?"

Completely unselfconscious, he strode across the navy and tan rug to the bed and turned back the covers on the other side. "What does it look like I'm doing? I'm coming to bed."

"You mean...you're going to sleep here? With me?"

"Where else would I sleep? You're my wife. Anyway, this is my bedroom."

Her gaze darted wildly around. Dear Lord, she should have realized. The large room, done in shades of burgundy, navy and tan and furnished with a massive armoire and chest of drawers that matched the headboard on the king-size bed was elegant and neat as a pin, but decidedly masculine.

The mattress dipped, giving her a start, and her head whipped around in time to see Dillon climb into the bed beside her.

Emily swallowed hard. "Uh...Dillon, you said... that is...I..."

After calmly adjusting the covers he turned on his side, propped up on one elbow and gave her a long, heated look. "Relax, will you? For Pete's sake, I'm not going to jump your bones. However, I do intend to start this marriage as I mean for it to go on. And that means sharing a bed. Anyway, I have no intention of letting you sleep alone. What if you need my help during the night? It only makes sense for me to sleep here."

"I...I guess you're right."

"Good. I'm glad that's settled." Dillon leaned over and kissed her cheek. "Good night, Emily. Wake me if you need anything."

"I...I will. Good night, Dillon."

He turned over, punched his pillow into a different shape, then turned out the bedside lamp and settled into a comfortable position.

Long after Dillon's breathing had slowed to a steady rhythm Emily lay awake, staring through the darkness at the ceiling, her entire body taut as a drawn bow, acutely aware of him.

To her chagrin, even though at least two feet separated them on the enormous bed, she could feel his heat all along her right side, could hear him breathing. She squeezed her eyes shut. Heaven help her, she could even smell him, and the clean masculine scent filled her with a shameless longing.

It was embarrassing. And humiliating.

Especially since it was evident that he was not in the least bothered by any such lustful thoughts about her. Here she lay, all hot and bothered, and he'd fallen asleep within minutes of turning out the light. He may claim that she bore no resemblance to a whale, but apparently he found her about as alluring as one.

Sweet heaven, how he wanted her. Dillon lay on his side, facing away from Emily, wide awake, every cell in his body aching for her. She was so damned beautiful. And he loved her so much.

She sighed, and the bed rocked gently as she shifted positions. Dillon squeezed his eyes shut and gritted his teeth. Damn. He hadn't known that sharing a bed with her would be both heaven and hell.

He still felt like pinching himself. He couldn't believe it. After years of hopeless yearning, the impossible had happened. Emily was his. His wife.

And she was pregnant with his child.

He frowned into the darkness as guilt stabbed him. It had been wrong to marry her without telling her about the baby. He knew that. She deserved to know the truth, especially before taking such a step. But what else could he have done?

He had meant to tell her. He really had. But how could he? It was important that Emily remain calm. Dr. Conn had warned that undue stress or upset could throw her into premature labor and the baby could be in trouble. Telling her the truth now was a risk he simply could not take.

When the time was right, he would tell her, he vowed. No matter the consequences. He could only hope that by then he would have won her love.

In the meantime, though, she was his.

His mouth twisted wryly as he thought of the many platonic nights ahead of him. Damn. It was going to be the purest, most excruciatingly delicious hell any man ever endured.

Chapter Eleven

Emily slapped her cards down, face up. "Gin!" she crowed, then laughed with delight when Dillon scowled.

"What? Dammit, that's the fifth game in a row you've won." He narrowed his eyes. "Something's fishy here."

She fluttered her eyelashes and smiled with exaggerated innocence. "Why, Dillon. Are you accusing me of cheating?"

"Are you?"

"Don't be ridiculous. I'm just a better player than you, that's all."

He gave a rude snort. "Yeah, right. That'll be the day."

"Okay, if you're such a hotshot player, prove it." She slid the cards across the small table that he'd placed in front of the sofa. "Deal."

"Oh, no you don't. I told you that was going to be the last hand. I have work to do."

"Please, Dillon, just one more game," she wheedled. "That's all. I promise."

"Uh-huh. That's what you said before the last one. And don't give me that doe-eyed look. It's not going to work this time. I—"

The doorbell chimed, surprising them both. "Who can that be?" Frowning, Dillon rose and went to answer the summons.

From her position, reclining on the living room sofa, Emily could not see into the foyer, but when Dillon opened the door she heard a lilting female voice.

"Hello, darling. May I come in?"

"Actually, Pam—"

"I called your office but apparently that assistant of yours didn't give you my message, so I decided I'd just drop by."

"Pam, there's something—"

"I knew you wouldn't mind."

The woman's voice had suddenly grown more distinct, and Emily realized that she had brushed past Dillon and entered the apartment without waiting for his permission. The sound of stiletto heels on the marble floor of the foyer told Emily that she was now heading her way.

"But really, darling, you ought to fire that old witch. She takes entirely too much on herself. It's impossible to get through to you with her screening your ca—"

Spotting Emily, the blonde jerked to a halt in the arched doorway to the living room.

"Oh! I'm sorry. I didn't realize that Dillon had

company.'' As the woman's gaze ran over Emily's ripe figure a calculating gleam entered her eyes, and after the briefest hesitation she smiled and started forward again with her hand outstretched.

''I'm Pamela Morris, a close friend of Dillon's,'' she announced, placing a subtle but unmistakable emphasis on the word *close.* ''And you are...?''

''Emily. Emily Maguire.''

By nature, Emily was a friendly person, but for some reason she disliked Pamela Morris on sight, and it gave her immense pleasure to witness the shock that raced over the woman's perfectly made-up face.

''Maguire?'' she repeated in an incredulous voice. Emily could almost see the wheels begin to turn in the woman's head. ''Ah, then you must be a relative of Dillon's.''

''Wrong,'' he drawled. ''Emily's my wife.''

''Your *wife!*''

''That's what I tried to tell you before you barged in.''

Snapping her gaping mouth shut, Pamela folded her lips into a thin line. She narrowed her eyes and looked from Dillon to Emily, then back, and snapped, ''She's pregnant.''

''Very observant.''

''Is that how she tricked you into marrying her? By getting herself knocked up? Good grief, Dillon, I can't believe you fell for that. Don't you know that's the oldest trick in the book? Trust me, both as a woman and an attorney, I know.''

The look that came over his face was so black and murderous that Emily cringed back on the sofa. Glittering a lethal, icy blue, his gaze stabbed into the woman like twin knives.

Pamela seemed oblivious to the fury she had unleashed, which amazed Emily. Was the woman insane? Or just plain stupid? Emily knew with certainty that if he ever looked at her that way she would run for her life.

"That's it," he growled. "Get out."

"What? Ow! Dillon, what are you doing?" Pamela cried when he clamped his hand around her upper arm and began to frog-march her toward the door.

"You're leaving. Now."

"No, Dillon, listen to me. How do you know that's even your baby she's carrying? No, wait! I—"

The door slammed with enough force to rattle the pictures on the wall. Emily winced. The air seemed to throb with the sudden silence.

Dillon stalked back into the living room, still simmering. When his gaze met Emily's his mouth twisted sheepishly. "Sorry about that."

He was so obviously uncomfortable that her mood instantly brightened. Why, he's embarrassed, she thought.

Dillon looked at her with concern. "Are you okay? I hope she didn't upset you."

"Oh, I'm fine."

"Good." Obviously unwilling to discuss what had just occurred, he walked into the adjoining dining room, where he'd spread out a set of blueprints and a folder containing the specs for a new high-rise to be built along the Hempstead highway.

As Dillon turned his attention to the documents Emily studied him, an odd, sweet tightness in her chest.

She was happy, she realized. Happier than she'd ever been, and it was all because of this man.

The three weeks since their wedding had been a revelation.

Intimacy between a man and a woman, she'd learned to her great amazement, did not necessarily require lovemaking. It could blossom and grow quite naturally and beautifully under the right conditions, no matter how platonic.

Her road to that discovery had begun on her wedding night.

Awakening an hour or so after drifting off, she'd been amazed that she'd fallen asleep at all, but a desperate need to visit the bathroom had prevented her from pondering how that had happened.

She'd tried to ease out of bed without disturbing Dillon, but for the last couple of months her enormous girth had made any movement, particularly from a reclining position, a struggle. After she'd squirmed and scooted for only a moment or so, Dillon had rolled out of bed, come around to her side and hauled her up.

Ignoring her assurances that she could manage the rest of the way on her own, he'd steadied her as she'd waddled to the bathroom, and when she'd come out a few minutes later he'd been there, waiting just outside the door to help her back into bed.

Twice more during their first night together as man and wife, and two or three times every night since, the routine had been repeated. Though at first she'd felt awkward and embarrassed, the simple helpful gesture had initiated another subtle but inexorable shift in their relationship.

Of course, Emily realized there was a strong physical attraction between her and Dillon. At first she'd thought it was one-sided on her part, that she was imagining things, but before long not even his habitual stern expression could hide the banked fire in his eyes whenever he looked at her.

Given her condition and their history, Emily found that amazing, but the fact remained that whenever they were together the very air around them seemed to crackle with electricity.

However, it was more than chemistry that had brought about this delightful change. It was the thoughtfulness that came so naturally to Dillon, his absolute commitment to her and the baby, his strong sense of responsibility.

And it was the little things, the small, everyday kindnesses—a glass of juice and her prenatal vitamin on the bedside table when she awoke each morning, the way he telephoned her every hour or so from the job site throughout the day, the daily, detailed instructions he gave to Mrs. Taggert about her care, a blanket tossed over her at night while she slept.

Though Emily knew that Dillon's main concern was the baby, he seemed genuinely interested in her well-being, as well.

Since their marriage three weeks ago he'd spent every moment away from the job with her, not leaving in the morning until Mrs. Taggert arrived, and always returning home before time for the housekeeper to leave.

He pampered her outrageously. To keep her occupied, he brought her puzzles and books and needlepoint projects or anything else she requested. He was remarkably patient with her mood swings, and when she grew cranky and tired of looking at the four walls of the bedroom, he carried her to the living room for a change of scenery, as he'd done that evening.

Each night he brought dinner to her on a tray and ate his own on a small table next to the bed or sofa, wherever she lay. Afterwards they would play cards or watch television together, or some evenings he would simply sprawl out beside her on the king-size bed and they would talk. To her surprise, she'd discovered that she could discuss almost anything with Dillon.

It was funny, Emily mused. During those quiet conversations they'd learned more about each other than they had in all the years since they'd met.

She'd told him about her early childhood with her elderly grandparents and her mother's infrequent visits—how unsettling they had been for her, how heart-rending it had been when she inevitably took off again for parts unknown. Emily told him of being shuffled from one relative to another after her grandparents had died, and how unwanted and in the way she'd felt. None of her relatives had wanted another mouth to feed, and at eighteen, she had struck out on her own.

The drudgery of the four years that had followed, when she had worked a series of menial jobs to get through college, she glossed over and concentrated instead on explaining what big plans she'd had.

She had gotten a degree in education and had planned to join the Peace Corps for a couple of years before settling down in a stateside teaching job.

Then, just months before graduating, two things happened; her mother showed up, gravely ill with cancer and seeking her help, and she met Keith. Soon all of her plans had gotten lost in that first dizzying flurry of falling in love.

Dillon told her of his struggles to start his business,

of how Gert and her late husband, Carl, had encouraged him. Gert had immediately volunteered to do his clerical work, and she and Carl had helped him get his first loan to set up an office and buy the tools and heavy equipment he'd needed. They'd even let him live with them, rent free, until the business began to show a steady profit.

Seeing her opportunity, Emily asked the question that she'd wondered about for a long time. "Wouldn't it have been easier if you had gone to college and gotten a degree in say…oh…architecture or engineering before starting your company?"

"Sure. But it didn't work out that way."

"Why not?"

Dillon shrugged. "There wasn't any money for me to attend college."

"What? But that can't be. Keith told me about the college fund your father set up for all of you. That money put both Charlotte and Keith through college. Why not you?"

"After Charlotte graduated, I was all set to start college, but that summer Dad had a heart attack and died. Keith was a junior in high school at the time. Two days after Dad's funeral, Mother informed me that Keith wanted to become a doctor, and since that was going to be expensive, she was earmarking the remainder of the fund exclusively for his education."

"That's *terrible!* And so unfair! How could she?"

"Hey, it was never any secret that Keith was her favorite. Anyway, as it turned out, she was right. He ran through the entire fund before he finished his studies." Dillon's mouth quirked. "Even back then he was lousy with money. Never could live within his means.

"By then my business was beginning to take off, so I paid for his last year of med school and subsidized him financially during his internship."

"Really? He never told me that." But then, he wouldn't, she realized, given Keith's competitive attitude toward his brother. He would have hated anyone knowing that he was in any way beholden to Dillon.

She looked at him quizzically. "Now I'm even more surprised at your mother's attitude. I mean, given how she felt about Keith, you'd think she'd be more appreciative of what you did for him."

Dillon fixed her with one of his penetrating looks and shook his head at her naivete. "You really are a dreamer, aren't you? She thought it was the least I could do."

And so, probably, had Keith, Emily now realized, watching Dillon from across the room as he worked.

Every now and then he stopped reading long enough to punch some numbers into a pocket calculator and jot down something, but otherwise he was totally absorbed in the proposal he was working up.

Behind that tough exterior and blunt manner, was a razor-sharp intellect and a surprisingly wry sense of humor, Emily had come to realize. Why had it taken her so long to discover that?

The baby gave a tremendous kick, and Emily jumped. Out of the corner of his eye Dillon must have seen, because he looked up. "Are you okay?"

"I'm fine. I think the baby just wanted me to change positions."

At that moment the grandfather clock chimed eleven. Tossing his pencil aside, Dillon rose and walked to the sofa. "Time for bed," he announced and scooped her up.

Looping her arm around his shoulders, Emily settled back in his embrace. His great size and strength no longer intimidated her. Now she reveled in it. She had come to adore the breadth of those shoulders, the solid feel of him, his warmth. Drawing in a deep breath, she inhaled his scent deep into her lungs, and felt smugly secure and happy.

As he carried her down the hallway she studied his profile, and was seized by a sudden imp of mischief. A sly grin curved her mouth, and she chuckled softly.

Dillon turned his head, his gaze finding hers. "What's so funny?"

"Oh, nothing," she replied in a butter-wouldn't-melt-in-her-mouth tone. "I was just wondering how many more of them I can expect."

"How many more of what?"

"Your women. I mean, let's see." She held up one hand and began ticking off names on her fingers. "So far there's been your real estate agent friend, Lois Neeson. Then there was that socialite, Eileen Rogers, now Ms. Morris." She smiled and added sweetly, "A lady lawyer, no less. I must say, I'm impressed with your standards. Not a bimbo in the lot. So far, anyway."

Dillon narrowed his eyes. "Why, you little devil. You're enjoying this, aren't you?"

"Who? Me?" Unable to keep a straight face any longer, she dissolved into a fit of giggles.

"I'm glad you find my life so amusing," he drawled.

"Hey. When you're big as a whale, confined to bed

and cooped up in one room all day you take your fun where you find it."

"Yeah, well, go ahead and laugh." He bent and placed her on the bed, but instead of straightening he remained leaning over her. Bracing his hands on either side of her shoulders, he brought his face to within an inch of hers, so close she could feel his breath feathering over her skin, smell the lingering scent of the wine he'd had with dinner.

Emily's own breathing shut down. Belatedly, as her heart began to pound, she wondered at her own temerity. Only a fool would tweak a tiger's tail.

Then she realized that it wasn't anger she saw in Dillon's eyes. The sizzling look sent a thrilling little shiver of excitement skipping through her.

A slow smile curved his mouth, and his voice dropped to a dangerous, sexy rumble. "You're safe now. But just remember, little one. You won't be pregnant much longer. After this baby arrives and the doctor says you're recovered, you're gonna pay. Big time."

During the next couple of weeks, every time Emily thought of Dillon's rumbled threat, which was often, she felt tingly all over. She was giddy as a schoolgirl, existing in a constant state of delicious anticipation.

Emily had plenty of time to think about her reaction and analyze her feelings, although it did not take long. Self-deception was not one of her failings. As improbable and unbelievable as it seemed, the reason for her bubbly euphoria was inescapable; she had fallen in love.

Completely, deeply, head over heels in love with a

tough, somber man whom she had thought of as her enemy until only a few months ago.

She tried to tell herself it was a hormonal thing, something she could chalk up to her pregnancy, or that it was just boredom or loneliness. After all, except for Mrs. Taggert popping into her bedroom every once in a while to see if she was okay, she spent her days alone in one room, but she knew she was grasping at straws.

Even when she merely whispered the admission in her mind it sounded crazy, but she knew it was true. She loved Dillon.

Whether or not he loved her, she didn't know. Probably not, she accepted with a little twinge of regret, but she refused to let herself become discouraged.

Because, amazingly, he wanted her. Even as misshapen and huge as she was, Dillon sometimes looked at her as though she was the sexiest, most desirable woman on the planet. That gave her hope, for she knew that, with a bit of luck, desire that strong could turn to love.

The wait for the baby's arrival, which had been tedious before, now seemed impossibly long, each day dragging by like a sloth on tranquilizers.

If only, instead of Keith, it had been Dillon who had asked her out all those years ago, Emily mused as she whiled away each day in bed, counting the minutes until Dillon returned. How different her life would have been.

Inevitably her thoughts drifted back to that day in the hospital cafeteria when she had met the dashing Dr. Maguire and his stern older brother. Would she have gone out with Dillon, had he asked her? she wondered.

Emily's mouth twisted. Probably not, she admitted, chagrined at her own youthful lack of judgement. At twenty-one she would have chosen flash over substance. She'd been so captivated by Keith's charm and glib tongue that she had barely given Dillon a second look.

But then, who would have thought that she could find the love and happiness, the contentment and sense of belonging that she'd always longed for with such a somber, tough man?

With a happy sigh, Emily lay back against the mound of pillows propped against the bed's headboard and smiled. She was truly happy, happier than she had ever imagined she could be. Suddenly, for the first time, everything was going absolutely right in her life. She was married to a wonderful man whom she adored. He had provided her with a lovely home and more financial security than she'd ever dreamed of having. And soon—very soon, she thought, rubbing her palms over the swollen mound of her belly—she was going to have a baby.

She smiled dreamily, savoring the glow of contentment that made her feel warm and tingly all over. Yes, life was good.

Not even the thought of how angry Adele was going to be when she returned and found out about the baby and her and Dillon could dampen Emily's spirits. Well…not much, anyway.

That optimistic belief, however, was shattered later that same evening when she discovered just how much destructive fury her mother-in-law was capable of unleashing.

Dillon had come home early to take her for her weekly appointment with Dr. Conn. On returning, the instant he carried her inside the apartment Emily balked at returning to bed and insisted on spending the evening on the sofa.

"I don't know. Going to the doctor always wears you out. Maybe you should go to bed and rest."

"All I do is rest. Anyway, I'm sick to death of that bed. Please, Dillon."

One look at her pouty mouth and pleading eyes and he caved. "Oh, all right. Since the checkup went so well, I guess it won't hurt."

He settled her on the sofa and covered her with a light throw. "I'll go see what Mrs. Taggert prepared for dinner," he announced and turned to head for the kitchen. He'd barely taken two steps when the doorbell chimed.

Dillon and Emily exchanged a look, and she rolled her eyes. "Don't tell me I'm going to have to fend off another irate ex-lover."

"Very funny. Just keep it up. You're racking up a heavy tab."

Oh, Lord, she hoped so, Emily thought gleefully as she watched him stride out of the room. He was so masculine and sexy just looking at him made her heart go pitty-pat. The thought of making love with him darn near melted her insides.

Her smile collapsed at Dillon's first word.

"Mother. You're ba—"

The crack of Adele's palm against his cheek was unmistakable, causing Emily to jump. "You disgusting pig," Adele spat, her voice quivering with rage.

A couple of seconds of stunning silence followed, during which Emily's instinctive reaction was to go to Dillon's aid. Without thinking, she tossed aside the soft throw and swung her legs over the side, but every time she tried to push to her feet she fell back again.

Then from the foyer came Dillon's sardonic drawl. "From that loving greeting I take it that you know."

"Yes, I know everything. Now get out of my way."

Emily heard Adele's angry footsteps cross the foyer seconds before she stomped into the living room. Dillon followed on her heels, and Emily's eyes widened when she spotted the red imprint of Adele's hand on his left cheek.

"There you are." Her mother-in-law stopped in the middle of the Oriental rug and glared at her with so much hatred she shrank back against the sofa cushions. "You little slut."

"All right, that's enough," Dillon growled. "You can say whatever you like to me, but you will not come into my home and speak to my wife that way. I won't allow it."

Adele swung on him. "Your wife," she sneered, her lips curled with revulsion. "*You* won't allow it. Ha! Why, you're nothing but trash. Just like I always said you were.

"How *dare* you sneak around behind my back and seduce Keith's wife into marrying you? That fool girl probably believes you actually care about her, but we both know that you're just trying to take over Keith's child. Well, I won't have it." She advanced on him a step and poked his chest with her finger. "Do you hear me? You're not fit to raise my son's child."

"Adele, please, can't we discuss this civilly?" Emily pleaded.

The other woman swung back to her like an enraged tigress. "And as for you! How dare you not tell me you were expecting my grandchild?" she snarled, ignoring her question.

Wide-eyed, Emily stared up at her, her mouth suddenly dry. She'd never seen anyone so angry before—not even Adele. "I...I know I should have. But...well...at first you were so broken up about Keith, then before I had a chance to say anything you left for Florida."

"You could have called and told me. I would have flown back at once."

Which was precisely why I didn't, Emily thought. "I know. You're right. But...well...I thought you needed the time away, and since there was nothing you could do—"

"I could have saved you from marrying him!" she snapped, casting a nasty look Dillon's way. "I know you married him because you couldn't work any longer and you needed someone to look after you. Of course, if you hadn't squandered Keith's money, that wouldn't have been necessary. However, for the sake of my grandchild, I would have taken you in and supported you."

Emily shuddered at the thought.

"Since you appear to know so much, would you mind telling me how you came by your information?" Dillon asked.

"I called your office to tell you I was back."

"If you're claiming Gert told you, I don't believe it."

"No. It was the new girl. The one who took Emily's place. When I identified myself she told me that you had taken your wife, *Emily,* to see her obstetrician because her baby was due in a week. Then she practically gushed about how wonderful she thought you were for coming to Emily's rescue and how romantic she thought the whole thing was.'' Adele smiled nastily. ''The stupid girl was a font of information. By the time I'd finished talking to her I knew every revolting detail.''

She turned to Emily, her expression accusing and contorted with revulsion. ''How could you? No matter how desperate you were, after being married to my precious Keith how *could* you bring yourself to marry Dillon? How can you bear to let him touch you?''

''Adele!'' Emily cried, shocked to her soul. ''How can you say such horrible things. For heaven's sake! Dillon is your son, too. Your own flesh and blood.''

Like a spark to tinder, Emily's words snapped something inside Adele, sending her temper blazing out of control. Her face twisted into a hideous mask of hatred and she bared her teeth in a feral snarl. ''That's just it. Dillon is *not* my son.''

Chapter Twelve

Emily gasped. She gaped at her mother-in-law, appalled.

Dillon's face wore its usual stoic expression.

"Adele, how can you say such a horrible thing?" Emily chastised when she'd regained her breath. "That's low, even for you."

"How *dare* you judge me. You know nothing. *Nothing.*"

"I know that the way you treat Dillon is abominable," Emily fired back, her own temper beginning to come to a boil. "I know that you've always favored Keith over him for no good reason. I know that while you spoiled your younger son rotten you were verbally and emotionally abusive to your older son. That's inexcusable."

"Let it go, Emily," Dillon advised in a weary

voice. "It doesn't matter. It's not like this is anything new."

"It matters to me. I'm not going to sit by quietly while she denies her own flesh and blood."

"You stupid, *stupid* girl," Adele hissed. "Don't you understand? *He is not my son!*"

Dillon's head jerked back. He grew utterly still, his gaze narrowing warily on the older woman.

"But that's...that's crazy," Emily stammered, taken aback. "For heaven's sake, Adele, he and Keith were often mistaken for twins."

"Because they shared the same father," Adele said bitterly. "My husband had an affair with one of his students after Charlotte was born. I don't know how long it went on. The first I knew of the affair was when Colin walked into our home with his two-day-old infant son in his arms. The little tramp he'd been sleeping with had died in childbirth.

"He begged me with tears streaming down his face to accept the child and let everyone think he was ours. Colin knew he'd be dismissed from the university if the truth got out."

"And you went along with that?" Dillon demanded.

"I had no choice," she snapped. "Colin had desperately wanted a son. Now that he had one he couldn't bear the thought of giving you up for adoption.

"When Charlotte was born there were complications, and afterwards there was some doubt as to whether I would ever have another baby. I was afraid if I refused to accept you I would lose Colin." She glared at Dillon, her face twisted with distaste and loathing. "Believe me, if I'd known then that I would have Keith two years later I never would have agreed to raise that little slut's bastard.''

''Yeah, well, it's too bad you weren't clairvoyant. You would have done both of us a favor if you'd refused.''

''Oh, Adele,'' Emily murmured sadly. ''How could you not love an innocent little baby? It's not as though what happened was Dillon's fault.''

The rebuke only made her mother-in-law more angry. ''You try dealing day after day with a living reminder of your husband's infidelity and see how loving and nurturing you'll be.''

All Emily could do was shake her head, saddened to her soul by Adele's bitter vindictiveness. No wonder Dillon was somber and often remote. That hard shell he'd built around himself was his only defense. She shuddered to think what his life would have been like if he hadn't had Gert.

''All these years the mere sight of you has brought me pain,'' Adele spat, turning her attention to Dillon once again. ''As if that weren't bad enough, now you're trying to steal my son's child. Well, you won't get away with it. The first thing tomorrow, I'm going to consult an attorney.''

She spun around and stomped toward the door. Once there, she stopped and sent them one last hate-filled look. ''You haven't heard the end of this.''

Her footsteps clacked across the marble floor of the foyer and the door slammed with a crack like a gunshot.

Emily's gaze locked on her husband. He was staring at the empty arched doorway through which Adele had just disappeared. His face looked as though it had been carved from granite. Watching him, Emily felt as though someone had just cleaved her heart in two with a dull ax. What must he be feeling?

"Oh, Dillon, I'm so sorry."

He turned his head only slightly and looked at her out of the corner of his eye. His mouth kicked up at one corner in a crooked smile that did not reach his eyes. "What for? It's not as though I've lost anything." He went to the drinks tray and poured himself a bourbon and water, then returned and sank down in the chair next to the sofa and took a sip. "Actually, I'm glad I found out. Now at least I know why she hates me."

"Still...to learn that way...with her spewing so much venom. It must have been just awful for you."

"Is that what you're fretting over?" He smiled at Emily's troubled expression. "Hell, sweetheart, I'm used to that sort of thing. To tell you the truth, it's a relief to know that she's *not* my mother."

"Are you sure?"

"Positive." He looked her over and frowned. "I'm just sorry she upset you. Are you okay?"

Emily bit her lower lip. "Well...I am a bit worried about her consulting an attorney. Do you think she'll try to get custody of the baby?"

"Knowing Moth—" He grimaced. "Knowing Adele, I wouldn't put it past her, but any reputable attorney will tell her she doesn't have a case. You're the baby's natural mother, and there's no way she can prove you unfit."

"You really think so?" At his nod she exhaled a long breath. "Oh, good. Good."

"However, I should warn you, in recent years there's been more consideration given by the courts to grandparents' rights. It's a safe bet she'll sue for court ordered unsupervised visitation."

"What!" In an instinctive, protective gesture, Emily splayed both hands over the turgid mound of her belly. "She can *do* that?" At Dillon's nod, she groaned. "I was going to allow Adele to see the baby, of course, but not alone. I don't want her to have that much influence on my child."

"Hey, relax. It's not going to happen, I promise. I'll give her an hour or so to cool off, then I'll go talk to her. Provided you promise not to budge from this sofa while I'm gone. What I have to say won't take long."

"I'll stay right here. But, Dillon, what good will it do to go over there? She won't listen to you."

"Just trust me, okay? Believe me, there won't be any lawsuit."

"How do you know?"

"I know." *Because when Adele finds out that I'm the father and not Keith, she won't want to have anything to do with your baby,* he added silently.

The discussion with Adele went much as Dillon expected. Spotting him through the peephole in her front door she at first refused to open the door.

"Go away. I have nothing more to say to you," she called through the panel.

"Yeah, well, I have something to say to you. Open up Adele." He waited a moment. When she didn't answer he added, "Look, this won't take long. Now, we can have this discussion here, or I can come to the university and embarrass you in front of your students and colleagues. I don't think you want that. One way or another though, we're going to talk. When and where, is up to you.''

Another silence, then the lock clicked and the door opened. Shooting him a sullen look, Adele stepped back and waved him inside. She marched into the living room of her elegant little town house, her silk caftan fluttering around her ankles. When she reached the middle of the Oriental rug she whirled around and faced him with her arms crossed tightly beneath her breasts. Her eyes glittered with anger and dislike. ''Well?''

''I'm here to advise you against taking any legal action to gain access to Emily's baby. Believe me, you really don't want that.''

Adele tossed her head back and laughed scornfully. ''Oh, you'd like that, wouldn't you? Well, forget it. There's no way you can keep me from Keith's child.''

''It isn't Keith's child Emily is carrying. It's mine.''

The bald statement snapped her head back as though he'd slapped her. ''I don't believe you!''

''Nevertheless, it's true.''

''You mean the two of you had an affair behind Keith's back?'' she cried in outrage.

''No, of course not.'' Dillon held up both hands to stave off the explosion he could see coming. ''Listen to me. Keith was sterile.''

''What?'' She narrowed her eyes. ''You're lying. He would have told me.''

''Hardly. That's not something a guy goes around telling his mother. Especially not a guy with an ego like Keith had. Anyway, since we were brothers he asked me to donate sperm for in vitro so that Emily's baby would carry at least some of his genetic makeup.'' Deliberately he didn't mention Keith's plan to pass the baby off as his own, or that Emily did not know about the switch.

Adele shook her head, but he saw the desperation building in her eyes. ''No. No, I don't believe you. You're just trying to keep me from my grandchild.''

Dillon shrugged. ''You don't have to take my word for it. Check with the clinic. Doctor-patient confidentiality doesn't extend beyond a patient's death, so you can petition the courts to see Keith's file. As for Emily, they won't give you access to her medical records, but I'm sure she'll allow the doctor to confirm that she had in vitro.''

As he had hoped, his willingness for her to have the information convinced her. He watched her sag with defeat, her last shred of hope drifting away like a puff of smoke in the wind. She sank down on the edge of the sofa and looked at him forlornly. ''Then...the baby isn't my grandchild.''

''That's right.'' He waited a beat to let that soak in, then asked, ''So, are we agreed that you won't be taking legal action?''

She darted him one last glare, but even that lacked its usual venom. Her head drooped forward and she covered her face with both hands. ''Yes. I have no interest in a child of yours.''

Her shoulders began to shake. At first she wept silently, but then gasps and long, piteous wails tore from her throat.

Despite everything, Dillon could not help but feel sorry for her. He would have gone to her and offered what comfort he could had he not known how much she would despise that. Instead, he left her to her sorrow and quietly let himself out.

Outside, he sat in his car for a long time, staring at the elegant town house, knowing this was the last time he would ever come there, and that he would probably never again see the woman whom he had all of his life believed to be his mother.

His gut was in turmoil, roiling with so many emotions at once he didn't know what he felt. There was sadness, of course, but there was also anger and frustration, and so many "if onlys" that it hurt to think about them.

Finally, he put the car into gear and drove away.

On the drive back to his apartment Dillon was deep in thought, his mind flashing back over the years, and he was filled with sadness at the useless pain and futility of it all.

At least he'd accomplished one thing tonight, he thought. He'd told Adele the truth and gotten her off Emily's case. Dillon's mouth flattened and he exhaled a long sigh. Now, all he had to do was tell Emily.

Soon, he vowed. After the baby came and she was back on her feet. Then he'd tell her. And hope for the best.

His beeper went off, startling him. He dug the electronic gadget out of his pocket and glanced at the telephone number in the display, and his heart jumped right up into his throat.

It was Emily.

He jerked up the car phone and punched the speed dial. She answered on the first ring.

"Dillon?"

"What's wrong?"

"It's...it's time. I'm in labor, and the pains...the pains are already t-two minutes a-apart. Oh! *Oh!*

Hurry, Dillon!'' She groaned, and the hair on the back of his neck stood up.

''Hang on, sweetheart. I'll be right there.''

He slammed the phone down, stomped the accelerator to the floorboard and held the horn button down in a steady blast.

Five minutes later Dillon screeched to a halt in the circular drive at the front of his high-rise building. Leaving the motor running, he bailed out of the truck almost before it came to a complete stop.

''George! Watch my truck!'' he yelled as he sprinted past the startled doorman.

''But, Mr. Maguire, you can't park there. It's against—''

''Dammit, man, my wife's in labor. Just watch the damned truck! I'll be right back.''

Responding to the urgency in Dillon's voice with the universal awe of all men when confronted with the imminent birth of a child, George snapped to attention. ''Yes, *sir,* Mr. Maguire. You got it.''

Luckily the elevator doors opened instantly. Dillon inserted his key and hit the express button and the cubicle shot upward toward the penthouse like a bullet, but even that was too slow for him. He cursed a blue streak every inch of the way.

Dillon burst into his apartment to find Emily in the midst of a hard contraction that had her drawn up in the fetal position clutching her belly, her eyes squeezed shut and her face contorted in agony. The sight and the horrible sound that tore from her throat nearly stopped Dillon's heart.

''Dear Lord!'' He rushed to her side and bent to pick her up, but she shook her head adamantly and signaled him to wait. When the pain finally subsided it left her white-faced and panting and drenched in perspiration. "I...I'm sorry."

"You should be. Why the hell didn't you tell me you were having contractions before I left?"

"I...I wasn't...th-then. My water broke about... about twe-twenty minutes ago and the...the pains started coming fast and furious."

"Wouldn't you know, the one and only time I leave you alone for a few minutes, this happens."

She clutched one of his hands when he reached for her again. "Oh, Dillon, when my water broke I ruined your beautiful sofa. I'm so sorry."

"*That's* what you're apologizing for? Don't worry about that. It doesn't matter." Dillon wanted to snatch her up, but he forced himself to lift her as though she were made of fragile glass.

"But your sofa—"

"Forget the damned sofa! I can always buy another one," he snapped, the terror he was trying to hide overwhelming him. He'd read all of her books on pregnancy. He knew that when the water broke and the pains were that close they didn't have much time.

He headed for the door with his precious burden as fast as he dared.

"Don't forget my bag," Emily reminded him.

Cursing vividly, Dillon detoured to their bedroom, snatched up the small valise and raced out of the apartment without bothering to lock the door behind them.

"Dammit to hell. This is all Adele's fault," he raged on the ride down in the elevator. "I knew she had upset you. If anything happens to you or the baby—"

"Dillon, calm down. I'm only a week early. This

probably would have happened even if she hadn't dropped by.''

He scowled at her, not in the least convinced.

George must have been keeping an eye on the floor indicator above the elevator doors. When Dillon stepped out of the cubicle with Emily the doorman was holding the main door open, then when they'd passed by he darted ahead and snatched open the passenger door on the truck.

''Thanks, George.'' Dillon carefully placed her into the passenger seat, then raced around the front of the truck, climbed behind the wheel and burned rubber all the way down the curved drive and careened out into the street with a screech of tires.

He made the twenty-five to thirty-minute drive from his apartment to the medical center in just over fifteen. He'd telephoned Dr. Conn during his mad race home, and several nurses and orderlies were waiting for them at the entrance to the E.R. They loaded Emily onto a gurney and raced inside, with Dillon running alongside, holding her hand. ''Just hold on, sweetheart. Hold on.''

''Don't worry. Dr. Conn and his team are already washed up and waiting,'' one of the staff yelled to reassure them.

At the double doors into the delivery room one of the nurses stepped in front of Dillon and put her hands on his chest to hold him back. ''I'm sorry, Mr. Maguire, but you'll have to wait here.''

''To hell with that!'' he roared. ''I'm going to be with my wife when our child is born! Now get out of my way.''

''I'm sorry, but I can't let you in there until you wash up and put on scrubs.''

Dillon glared at her. "Then show me where I can wash up."

"There's no time."

"*Now,* dammit!"

The young woman's eyes opened wide, but she nodded and led him to the scrub room.

It seemed to Dillon that all hell was breaking loose when he burst into the delivery room minutes later wearing latex gloves, a surgical mask and a sterile paper gown over his clothes.

Sitting on a rolling stool at the foot of the birthing table, Dr. Conn was snapping orders. The nurses around the table were hopping to do his bidding, all the while murmuring encouragement to Emily.

In the grips of a hard contraction, she was perspiring profusely, red in the face, every muscle in her body straining to push and at the same time hold in the scream that was keening at the back of her throat.

Dillon rushed to the head of the table, elbowed aside a nurse and took Emily's hand. "It's me, sweetheart. I'm here. You're doing great, honey. Just great. It won't be much longer." His gaze sought the doctor's for confirmation, and the other man nodded.

Dillon had never been afraid of anything in his life, but he was afraid now. Absolutely terrified that he would lose this woman who meant more to him than life itself.

The contraction passed and Emily collapsed back against the pillow, panting hard. "D-Dillon?"

"I'm here." He snatched a paper towel off the surgical tray and blotted her face. Even her hair was drenched with sweat. In only a few seconds she began to tense again.

"Oh! Oh!" Gripping Dillon's hand, she caught her

breath and clenched her teeth, her face screwing up as another pain followed hard on the heels of the last one.

"That's it, Emily. Push. Push," Dr. Conn advised in a calm voice. "That's the way. Good girl. You're doing fine."

Straining with all her might, Emily bore down so hard her face turned an alarming purple, and she squeezed Dillon's hand so hard he was sure bones were broken.

He stared at her agonized face.

"Ah, here we go. Okay now, just one more good push should do it."

A long chilling sound, somewhere between a growl and a scream, escaped from between Emily's clenched teeth and her head and shoulders lifted partway off the table as she screwed up her face and bore down again.

"Here we go. Here we go. And...you have yourselves a girl!" the doctor cheered as he caught the slippery infant in his gloved hands.

"She has a healthy pair of lungs, too," one of the nurses added with a laugh. "No need to swat this one."

As the baby's outraged cries filled the room Emily collapsed back on the table, laughing and crying all at once, utterly exhausted. Dillon blotted her face again and looked at her with awe, so overwhelmed he couldn't speak.

Then the doctor placed the naked, squalling infant on Emily's abdomen. "Mr. and Mrs. Maguire, meet your daughter."

"Oh. Oh, my sweet baby," Emily cooed, her ordeal already forgotten. She gazed at the babe with abject adoration, her face aglow. She glanced up at Dillon with a beatific smile and stars in her eyes. "Oh, darling, isn't she beautiful?"

Dillon's heart gave a hard bump. Darling? Did she realize what she had just called him? Or was she simply caught up in the emotion of the moment?

He swallowed hard and looked at his daughter. She was red and covered in birthing fluids and blood, her little face screwed up as she made her displeasure known. Dillon smiled. "Yes. She is beautiful." Unable to help himself, he leaned down and placed a lingering kiss on Emily's mouth.

When their lips slowly parted he pulled back just a few inches and looked into her eyes. Though startled, they swam with joy and wonderment and, unless he was mistaken, a touch of hope. "You're beautiful," he whispered.

Three days later Dillon took his wife and daughter, seven pounds, one ounce, Mary Kate Maguire, home. Gert was there when they arrived, along with Mrs. Taggert, who would be occupying the guest room for the next week or so to help out. Both women oohed and ahhed over the baby, so anxious to get their hands on her they were practically salivating.

While Gert and Mrs. Taggert squabbled over who got to hold her first, Dillon hustled Emily off to bed, insisting that she rest.

The day was hectic. Though he and Emily had thought they'd stocked the nursery with every conceivable thing they would need, twice that afternoon he had to race to the pharmacy for some indispensable item.

The baby cried what seemed to him an abnormal

amount of time, but Emily just laughed and forbade him to call the pediatrician as he wanted, assuring him that nothing was wrong, that all babies cried.

Dillon had not suspected that such a tiny scrap of humanity could be so demanding and keep four adults hopping, but Mary Kate did. When she wasn't sleeping, she needed to be fed or burped or changed, or walked or bounced or cuddled.

He did it all gladly, except for the feeding, since Emily was nursing, but by the end of that first day he was dragging and felt more exhausted than he did after an eight-hour shift of physical labor on a construction site.

Throughout the day several friends stopped by to get a peek at Mary Kate and drop off a gift. That evening Charlotte called to inquire how Emily and the baby were faring, but there was a certain constraint in her voice. His sister still wasn't comfortable with Dillon's marriage.

Finally, by ten that evening all their friends had gone and Mrs. Taggert had retired for the night. For the first time that day the apartment was quiet.

Dillon checked the door locks and turned out the lights as he made his way to the bedroom. Reaching the door to the master suite he jerked to a stop and drank in the picture before him, entranced.

Propped up in the bed, leaning back against a mound of pillows, Emily held Mary Kate to her breast. With a serene smile on her face, she watched the baby suckle and stroked her downy cheek with one finger.

Dillon's chest grew so tight he could barely draw breath. She looked like a Madonna.

He knew with absolute certainty that he would

carry this picture with him for the rest of his days. Emily was the essence of womanhood, gentle, nurturing, utterly feminine, her face aglow with unconditional love and joy.

It was all worth it, he realized. No matter what their future held, no matter what it cost him when he told her the truth, he would never regret giving her this happiness.

Settling with Mary Kate in the nursery's rocking chair, she unbuttoned her blouse. As the infant began to suckle and knead her breast with a tiny fist, Emily leaned her head against the chair's high back and gazed through the lace curtains at the sun-drenched terrace, rocking gently. Ironically, the two months since Mary Kate's birth had been both the most wonderful and most unbearable of her life, she mused. She had everything she had ever dreamed of and longed for...except an intimate relationship with the man she loved.

She had been happy before her daughter arrived, certainly, but always in the back of her mind she'd worried about Dillon, worried that he'd feel trapped and miserable, that her happiness and security were coming at the price of his.

He, after all, had married her out of an overactive sense of duty and responsibility, maybe with a little guilt for his brother's betrayal thrown in. Marriage and fatherhood had not been part of his life plan even as little as a year ago. Consequently, there had been that little niggling doubt in the back of her mind of how he would adjust to the enormous changes being a husband and father would bring to his life.

These last couple of months since the baby's birth, she had come to realize she had worried needlessly. Dillon had taken to fatherhood like a duck to water. From the moment that Mary Kate had made her noisy entrance into the world he had been smitten—almost comically so. And since then, the infant had wound him right around her tiny little finger.

Merely thinking about the way Dillon was with the baby made Emily smile. Each evening, the second he entered the apartment he tossed a burp cloth over his shoulder and picked her up. Mary Kate had become aware of her surroundings and the people who populated her world. Dillon loved it that she now recognized him and kicked and flailed her arms in excitement at the sight of him or even the sound of his voice.

Whenever he walked around the apartment with Mary Kate, Emily was always struck by the stark contrasts between them. She looked like a tiny doll, cuddled against Dillon's big body. His hand almost spanned her entire backside from her little diapered rump to her shoulders. A fuzz of dark hair covered her head, but her pink-and-white skin emphasized Dillon's dark coloring, just as her delicate little body emphasized his great size and strength.

To Emily's surprise, Dillon changed the baby's diapers, bathed her and burped her, and now that she had begun to eat a little cereal he insisted on being the one to feed her in the evening. He walked the floor with her when she was cranky, and those first weeks whenever she had woken for her 2:00 a.m. feeding it had been Dillon who had rolled out of bed, changed her and brought her back to their bed so that she could nurse.

He was so besotted, it was almost as though Mary Kate was his own daughter.

She could almost be jealous if she herself didn't receive so much attention from him, Emily thought.

Dillon never seemed to tire of her company or her conversation, and since Mary Kate's birth it seemed to Emily that he had begun to deliberately initiate physical contact with her.

It had begun with a back rub her first night home from the hospital, then he'd progressed to massaging her feet and calves and before she knew it she was receiving regular, full body massages. Emily shivered just thinking about how those powerful hands felt moving over her body.

In recent weeks, he had begun to touch her whenever possible—a companionable arm draped around her shoulders at pensive moments, like when they were viewing a sunset from the terrace or watching Mary Kate sleep, a hand on the small of her back or curved around her waist when they walked, a touch on her hair or arm when he passed by her. And more and more frequently now, a soft kiss hello and goodbye.

It was as though he was trying to accustom her to his touch.

Emily didn't know whether to laugh or scream. If that was, indeed, his intent, it was unnecessary. She was head over heels in love with him, and she urgently wanted him to touch her—to make love to her. She wanted that so much it was practically all she could think of. Couldn't he see that?

He wanted her, too. She knew he did. She could see it in his face whenever he looked at her. Those vivid blue eyes blazed at her with so much heat and hunger it was a wonder they both didn't go up in flames.

She had been so certain that he would attempt to consummate their marriage once she'd had her postnatal checkup. She'd made certain he knew the date of her appointment and that evening he had inquired how it had gone, but when she told him she'd gotten a clean bill of health from Dr. Conn he had nodded and given her one of his intense looks, but that was all.

She was beginning to suspect that he was waiting for her to make the first move. He *had* said that their marriage would not become a real one until she was ready.

Well, she was ready. She was *more* than ready; she was desperate.

It occurred to her that perhaps Dillon had something else on his mind. For the past couple of weeks it had seemed as though something was troubling him. He'd been preoccupied and more somber than usual, and several times she'd caught him staring at her intently, as though he was on the verge of confiding in her. About what, she had no idea.

If his business was in trouble or something of that nature, Emily hoped he would feel comfortable about discussing it with her, but so far he'd remained pensive and quiet.

Glancing down at her daughter, Emily smiled when she saw that Mary Kate had stopped nursing and was sound asleep, though periodically her little rosebud mouth made feeble sucking motions. Emily fastened her blouse, gently lifted the infant to her shoulder and coaxed a tremendous milky burp out of her, then placed her in her crib and covered her with a light receiving blanket.

Mary Kate fussed a bit, and Emily rubbed her back. As the baby settled, she gazed out the window again, a plan taking shape in her mind. Something had to be done if she and Dillon were ever going to achieve true closeness. She couldn't make him confide in her, neither did she have the nerve to come right out and ask him to make love to her, but there was more than one way to communicate.

Leaving her daughter sleeping, Emily hurried

across the hall to the master bedroom. The first thing she did was make a few calls, one of which was to Mrs. Taggert to ask if she could baby-sit.

The housekeeper had returned to her three-times-a-week schedule, but she, like everyone else, had fallen under Mary Kate's spell and was always eager to look after the baby. Emily had called on her to sit during the daytime on several occasions when she'd needed to run errands or keep an appointment, but never in the evening.

When all of her arrangements were made, Emily stripped out of her slacks and shirt and got to work.

An hour later she stood before the full-length mirror, surveying herself in the form-fitting little black dress and a pair of strappy high heels that were pure sin. The dress she had purchased before Keith's death, but had not had a chance to wear it until now.

Emily turned this way and that, a satisfied smile curving her mouth as she smoothed her palms down over her hips. She'd worked like a demon these past couple of months to regain her figure, but the results were well worth every ab-crunch, stair climb and leg-lift she'd sweated and panted through.

Tonight she'd taken special pains with her makeup, and with her auburn hair piled atop her head in artful disarray and the clingy little dress hugging every line of her body she looked pretty darn good for a twenty-nine-year-old new mom, she decided.

The doorbell rang, and Emily snatched up her small clutch bag and wrap and hurried to the door.

"Mrs. Taggert, thank you again for coming on such short notice."

"Oh, think nothing of it, my dear. You know I'm always happy to do it. Where is our little angel?"

"She's sleeping. I fed her about an hour ago, and there's enough expressed milk in the fridge for three more feedings, though she should only need two. Dillon and I won't be out that late. I've left the numbers where you can reach us by the telephone in the kitchen." She started to leave, then turned back. "Oh, by the way, Mary Kate doesn't like the bottle so she'll fuss, but she'll eventually take it."

"Now, now, don't you worry. I've raised three of my own. I can handle that little sweetie-pie. You and the mister just go out and have yourselves a real nice evening."

Emily couldn't help it; she blushed to the roots of her hair, but she managed a smile and a self-conscious "Thank you" before hurrying out.

If everything went as she'd planned, it was certainly going to be a memorable evening, she thought as she stepped onto the elevator.

Because it was rush hour it took Emily almost a half hour to make the fifteen-minute drive to the construction site. By the time she arrived most of the crew had gone. A few weary stragglers were still ambling over to the parking area from the construction site and several more were loading their tools.

Emily parked and checked her reflection in the mirror on the back of the visor. After powdering her nose and touching up her lipstick she took a deep breath and squared her shoulders, but as she started to get out of the car the office door opened and two people stepped outside—Dillon and Pam Morris.

Emily froze with her hand on the door handle. Pam hung on to Dillon's arm like a limpet and chattered away, laughing gaily every now and then. When they reached the bottom of the steps the woman put her palms flat on Dillon's chest and stepped close. Reaching up, she touched one crimson fingernail to his lips and smiled seductively. Dillon smiled back.

Emily's stomach did a slow, sickening roll.

Then the pain came. It seared through her like a hot knife and filled every cell in her body with a deep, aching hurt.

Hot on its heels came anger, striking full-force like a sledgehammer. But at least fury helped keep at bay the tears that threatened to spill over.

Absolutely furious, Emily restarted the car. It took every ounce of control she possessed not to floorboard the gas pedal and peel out of there like a bat out of hell, but that would attract Dillon's attention, which was the last thing she wanted. At the moment her husband was too entranced by the sexy lady lawyer to pay attention to yet another vehicle engine starting up, especially with all the workers leaving.

Emily was trembling and so upset she could barely put together a coherent thought. Dear Lord, what a fool she'd been, she silently raged as she merged in with the stragglers lining up at the exit, waiting their turns to jump out into the rush hour traffic. What a complete and utter fool.

No wonder Dillon hadn't been in any hurry to make love to her, she thought, furiously whipping up her anger to hold back the tears. Why should he? No doubt he was already getting all the action he could handle, what with his string of women.

To think, she had been so sure Dillon was an honorable man. Ha! Apparently the Maguire men all had some sort of hereditary infidelity gene, passed down from father to son. Thank heavens her baby had turned out to be a girl.

The worst part was, she hadn't seen it coming. Again. What was she? Some sort of magnet for lying, cheating husbands? God knew, Keith's final betrayal had nearly brought her to her knees, but Dillon's hurt a hundred times more.

In the past months she'd come to realize that her feelings for Keith had been those of an infatuated young girl, but she was a mature woman now, and she loved Dillon—or had—with every fiber of her being.

Grinding her teeth, Emily fought back tears. She would not fall apart over this, she vowed. She absolutely would not. At least, not now, while driving. She'd save her tears for later, when she was in the privacy of her home.

Which wouldn't be her home for much longer, she realized, biting back a sob.

She'd have to find a job right away. And an apartment. And a good daycare for Mary Kate. The thought of that made her tear up again. Emily could hardly bear the thought of someone else caring for her baby, of having to be away from her all day, five days a week, but she didn't see any other way.

The side of her fist slammed against the steering wheel hard enough to bruise. *Damn* you, Dillon Maguire! This is all your fault!

He was going to be upset over losing Mary Kate, but too bad. If he thought for a minute that she was going to put up with yet another philandering husband, he was crazy.

Mrs. Taggert was stunned when Emily let herself into the apartment.

"Why, Mrs. Maguire, what're you doing back?"

Emily managed a wan smile. "It turns out it was

a bad night to surprise my husband. He's, uh…he's meeting with someone."

"Oh, that's too bad."

You have no idea, Emily thought.

Disregarding Mrs. Taggert's protests, she paid her for the entire evening. As soon as the older woman had gone Emily called the restaurant and the hotel and canceled the reservations she had made earlier. So much for her big night of seduction, she thought as she hung up the telephone and headed for the master bedroom.

There she stripped out of her finery and donned a broomstick skirt and a scooped-neck knit top and wiped away most of the makeup she'd so carefully applied.

She was brushing out her fancy hairdo when the telephone rang. Emily shot the instrument a baleful look and let the answering machine pick it up. When she heard Dillon's voice she was glad she had.

"Hi. It's me. Sorry, Em, but I got a little tied up here, so I'm going to be late. I don't know how late, exactly, so don't wait dinner on me. If I get hungry I'll just grab something."

"I'll just bet you will," Emily muttered, glaring at the answering machine.

"Oh, and kiss Mary Kate for me. See you later, sweetheart." A click sounded, and the machine clacked and whirred and reset itself.

By the time Dillon arrived home it was almost nine. Emily had already bathed and fed the baby and put her to bed. She sat in a ball in the corner of the sofa, her arms wrapped around her up-drawn legs, her chin resting on her knees, staring into space, but when she heard Dillon's key in the lock she bolted for the kitchen.

Once there, she darted around, looking for something to do, and finally snatched a glass from the cupboard.

"Hey, anybody home?"

Ignoring his call, Emily opened the refrigerator and poured herself a glass of juice. She heard him call her name over and over, his voice fading as he disappeared down the hall toward the master bedroom. Emily sipped her juice and waited. It didn't take long.

"Ah, there you are."

Keeping her back to the door, she raised the glass and took another sip. She heard Dillon's footsteps cross the slate floor of the kitchen. The instant his hand touched her shoulder she turned away, breaking contact, and returned the juice carton to the refrigerator.

"Emily? What's wrong?"

"Nothing," she replied in a clipped voice, but she still did not look at him.

"You're not upset because I had to work late, are you?"

"No."

"I hope not. I try to keep regular hours and not let the business turn me into a workaholic, but once in a while things happen."

"I said I wasn't upset." Not about that, at any rate.

"Then why won't you talk to me?"

She shrugged. "I have nothing to say." Finishing the juice, she went to the sink and rinsed out the glass. She could feel Dillon's gaze boring into her.

"Have you had dinner?" he asked.

"No." She'd been too upset to eat.

"Me either. Why don't I order in something for us? How about some Chinese?"

Emily ground her teeth. It must have been a satisfying three hours if he hadn't taken time out to eat. "No, thank you."

"Then how about a pizza?"

"No. If you'll excuse me, I'm going to bed. It's been a long day." She headed for the door, but he sidestepped in front of her and blocked her path.

"C'mon, Emily," he coaxed. "You're not going to make me eat alone, are you?"

"If you want a dinner companion, I suggest you call Ms. Morris. I'm sure she'd be happy to oblige." The instant the words left her mouth she could have bitten her tongue off. She hadn't meant to say even that much yet. She had planned to give herself time to cool down, then discuss everything calmly and rationally.

"What? Where the hell did that come from?"

That he had the nerve to put on that innocent act infuriated her all the more, and she couldn't hold back any longer.

"Oh, don't pretend you don't know. I came by the job site today." She practically flung the words at him.

"You did? When?"

"At quitting time."

"Really? I'm sorry I missed you. I was probably over in the hard-hat area. You should have had Gert page me. Or at least waited for me."

Emily tipped her chin up. "You were at the office when I came by, but you were busy."

"I'm never too busy for—" He stopped, an arrested look coming over his face. ''Ah, now I'm beginning to get the picture. You saw Pam.''

''It was difficult not to. She was hanging all over you!'' Emily spat.

Dillon tipped his head to one side and studied her. Then, slowly, his eyes crinkled at the corners and a delighted expression spread over his face. ''Why, you're jealous.''

''I am no such thing.''

''All this time you've been razzing me about my past love life I thought you were joking, but you weren't. You're jealous.''

''You're not listening to me,'' Emily raged. ''I am *not* jealous. What I am is angry and fed up. And disgusted!''

''Uh-huh. And jealous.''

''Oh, for the— I've had enough of this. Get out of my way.''

She moved to go around him, but Dillon sidestepped in front of her again and grasped both of her arms.

''Let go of me.''

Instead of obeying the order he backed her up against the cabinets. ''Listen to me, Emily. If you think I'm having an affair with Pam, you're dead wrong.''

''Ha! Do you really expect me to believe that when I saw her plaster herself against you like a wet T-shirt? And why would she even drop by if you weren't involved? She knows you're married.''

''Right. And to someone like Pam that's like waving a red flag in front of a bull. But I made it clear that I wasn't interested. I told her I was in love with my wife.''

"Oh, sure. I'll just bet you turned down—" She blinked at him. "Wh-what?"

"I'm in love with you, Emily," he said in a deep rumble. He looked into her eyes, his own blazing with so much sincerity and emotion it was impossible not to believe him.

Overcome, Emily trembled as joy bloomed inside her. For a moment she could not speak for the aching tightness in her throat. Her eyes grew moist and her chin began to quiver. "Oh, Dillon, I love you, too," she finally choked out.

He closed his eyes, and his great shoulders sagged as his breath rushed out in a whoosh. "Thank God."

Then he snatched her close, and covered her mouth with his.

He had kissed her many times before, but never like this. In the past his kisses had filled her with trembling awareness, but each time she had sensed the steely control he was exercising, letting passions build just so far, and no further. Now all restraint was shattered.

Unleashed desire soared between them, wild and free. Without breaking the kiss, Dillon bent his knees, wrapped his arms around Emily and straightened, lifting her off the floor, held tight against his chest. She moaned and curled her arms around his neck and gave herself completely to the kiss.

For several moments they strained together in desperate hunger, while lips rocked insatiably and hearts pounded. Finally, their lips slowly parted.

Still holding Emily against his chest, Dillon's gaze roamed her face as though he could not believe she was truly his. "Dear Lord, how I love you," he whispered.

"Oh, my darling, you have no idea how happy that makes me." Framing his face between her palms, she gave him a trembling smile. "I love you, too. So much it hurts."

She angled her head and kissed him again, a long, lingering caress that fanned the flames of passion higher and higher until she could bear it no more. Breaking off the kiss, Emily buried her face against the side of his neck and murmured, "Take me to bed, my love."

Dillon stilled, and she felt a new tension in him.

"I want that too, but...Emily...first we need to talk. There's something—"

"No." Raising her head from his shoulder she looked into his eyes and shook her head. "I don't want to talk. Not now. We've done nothing but talk for months."

"But, Emi—"

She put four fingers over his mouth, cutting off his argument. "Please, Dillon. Tonight is special. Almost our wedding night. I don't want to discuss anything or answer any questions or hear any confessions about other women or past loves or anything else."

She leaned forward and touched the tip of her tongue to the corner of his mouth. "I just want to be with you," she whispered against his lips. She strung a line of tiny kisses along his jaw. "To touch and..." Catching his earlobe between her lips, she tugged it gently. "...be touched."

"Emily, listen to me. You don't understa— Ahhhh..."

She moved a bit higher and traced the intricate swirls with her tongue, then blew, filling his ear with her warm breath. A hard shudder shook Dillon's big frame all the way to his toes, and Emily smiled.

"I want to make love with you. I want to..." She mouthed his lobe again, then nipped "...feel you inside me."

The next instant the tip of her tongue plunged into his ear, and Dillon was lost.

With a low growl, he bent and hooked his arm under her knees and headed for their bedroom.

His long stride ate up the distance, and within seconds they were falling together onto the bed. Instantly their mouths fused in a rapacious kiss.

Hands clutched and roamed and clutched again. Bodies strained closer. Tongues entwined and darted, teeth scraped and nipped, lips rubbed and soothed.

Their hunger was enormous, built to a fever pitch by months of living together in chaste closeness.

"Sweet heaven, I want you," Dillon growled against her skin as he strung kisses over her collarbone.

"Oh, my love, I want you, too. Please, Dillon," she gasped. Clutching his hair in both hands, she turned her head restlessly from side to side on the pillow. "Oh, please. Please."

Springing up onto his knees, Dillon grabbed the gauzy skirt with both hands and jerked it down to her ankles and off and sent it sailing. He stilled briefly and stared, his hot gaze taking in his wife's long, shapely legs, the tiny scrap of black lace at the apex of her thighs, the delicate curve of her hips. Slowly, almost reverently, he placed his hand on her flat belly, his spread fingers spanning from one hipbone to the other.

Emily pressed her lips together and shifted. "I have stretch marks," she murmured self-consciously.

He leaned in for a closer look, and traced one thin, silvery line with his callused finger. "They only make you more beautiful."

Emily's belly quivered when his lips replaced his finger, and she closed her eyes and moaned, so unbearably touched and excited she thought she would surely faint.

The tiny sound renewed Dillon's urgency, and he pulled her to a sitting position, grasped the hem of her top and whipped it off over her head. Before it had joined the gauzy skirt in a puddle on the floor he unhooked the front clasp on her nursing bra and pushed the straps off her shoulders and arms. The instant her full breasts sprang free a drop of milk appeared on the tip of each rosy nipple.

Dillon's gaze shot up and met Emily's. She caught her lower lip between her teeth and felt heat spread over her chest and rise in her neck and face. "I...I should have warned you. Here, let me—" She reached to pull a tissue from the box on the bedside table, but he caught her wrist.

"No, don't." He met her startled eyes for a moment longer, then his gaze lowered to the two milky-white pearls. Slowly, he lowered his head, and Emily caught her breath as he took first one tiny bead, then the other onto his tongue.

Then his mouth closed around one nipple. Emily clutched his head with both hands, her own lolling back like a flower on a stem as a low keening groan slid from her throat.

In that small part of her brain that still functioned, she marveled at her body's reaction. Nursing Mary

Kate filled her with a warm glow, but Dillon's lips sent hot, excruciating pleasure through her entire body. Every sharp suction seemed to tug at her womb.

She cried out when Dillon suddenly abandoned her breasts and sprang off the bed. "Easy, sweetheart," he soothed.

Watching her all the while, he yanked off his shoes and socks and began to snatch off his clothes like a man possessed. Emily watched him avidly, enthralled, her body tingling with anticipation. Then, at last, he stripped off his briefs, and she caught her breath. He was fully aroused and magnificently male.

Bracing one knee on the edge of the bed, he bent and removed her sandals and stripped off her panties, sending the bit of lace sailing over his shoulder.

Then he was there, braced above her. His face was stiff and dark with passion, his eyes a blazing blue. "I wanted to go slow, but I don't think I can wait any longer."

Emily shivered at the rough passion in his voice. Smiling, she reached up and took hold of his shoulders with both hands. "I don't want you to." She tugged him downward and wrapped her legs around him. Her body quickened as she felt his manhood, nudging her. "Make love to me, Dillon," she whispered. "Now."

It was all the encouragement he needed. With one powerful stroke he entered her. Emily caught her breath and Dillon groaned and went perfectly still. His jaw clenched and he squeezed his eyes shut, savoring their oneness.

Soon, however, the age-old yearnings beckoned, and the movement began—a rhythm as old as time.

He loved her with every fiber of his being, with a

sureness and power that thrilled Emily to her very soul. She met every thrust, arching her hips eagerly to take him deep inside, grabbing greedily at the exquisite pleasure.

They were feverish, demanding, insatiable. The rapture quickly built upon itself, expanding and deepening until it could no longer be borne, and when the explosion came they cried out in unison and clung to each other as all around them the universe seemed to shatter in a blinding flash of white light.

Chapter Fourteen

The razor made a scraping sound as Dillon pulled it over his jaw, removing another strip of lather. His eyes were stern as they gazed at his reflection in the mirror. "Dammit, you are going to tell her. Today."

His mouth twisted. Yeah, right. That's what he'd been saying every day for the past month, and every day he'd come up with another excuse—nursing mothers should avoid stress, what they had was too new. They needed time to form a bond before he told her. He even tried to convince himself that she wouldn't want to know.

Dillon swished the razor through the stream of water coming from the faucet and scraped a swath through the lather on the other side of his face. The real truth was, he didn't want to tell her. Because he was terrified of losing her.

The past month had surpassed every fantasy he'd

ever had about what it would be like to be married to Emily, to wake up next to her every morning, to come home to her every night, to share his life with her. To make love to her. He was probably the happiest man alive—or at least, he would be if it weren't for the guilt that gnawed away at him constantly.

And it's going to continue to eat you alive if you don't tell her.

Completing the last stroke, he bent and splashed his face with water to rinse away the remaining globs of shaving cream, and patted his face dry. Over the edge of the towel his gaze connected to the one in the mirror and his mouth firmed.

Dammit, this couldn't go on. He would tell her tonight after dinner. No more excuses, he vowed silently.

Emily stumbled into the bathroom, and Dillon smiled as he watched her in the mirror. Damn. Even sleep-rumpled and with her eyes barely open she was gorgeous. "Good morning, sleepyhead."

"Mmm, morning." Slipping her arms around him from behind, she clasped her hands together over his middle, and pressed close. After planting several kisses along his spine she rested her cheek against his back and sighed.

Turning, Dillon leaned his hips back against the sink, looped his arms around her waist and pulled her between his spread thighs until they were nestled firmly together. He smiled, glorying in the casual intimacy, loving the feel of her.

"How about I take you out to dinner tonight, gorgeous?" He'd take her out dining and dancing, and when she was feeling relaxed and mellow he'd bring her home and confess everything.

"Mmm, that sounds wonderful. But we can't leave too early. I have to take Mary Kate to the pediatrician at four-thirty, and you know how it goes with doctors. If he's running late, it may be six-thirty or so before we get home, and then I'll need time to shower and change."

Dillon frowned. "What's wrong with her? Is she sick?"

"No. Nothing like that. This is just her three-month checkup. Also, she'll probably get her first immunizations."

"You mean shots?"

"Probably."

"That's settles it. I'm going with you."

Emily chuckled. "Dillon, that's not necessary. This is just routine stuff."

"Yeah, well...I'm still going. If they're going to poke my daughter with a needle I'm going to be there. I'll leave the site early and pick the two of you up around four."

Emily had to bite the inside of her cheek to keep from smiling as she watched her husband and daughter. Mary Kate had been weighed and measured, poked and prodded and examined thoroughly, and the whole time Dillon had hovered over her.

The baby had objected to the otoscope being stuck up her nose and in her ears and the tongue depressor had made her gag, all of which had earned the doctor scowls from Dillon. However, when the nurse stuck the needle into her little rump and she cut loose with a howl Emily had to grab his arm and hold him back.

He'd glared at the nurse, and the instant the baby's diaper was refastened he'd snatched her up and cuddled her close. Now, pacing the small treatment room, he jostled and patted and wiped away her piteous tears, all the while murmuring soothing nonsense and casting murderous looks at the pediatrician.

Ignoring him, Dr. Simpson addressed his comments to Emily. "She's doing just fine," he pronounced, scanning the notes he'd jotted down. "Her weight is normal for her size, no problems or abnormalities, and she's obviously healthy."

"That's good to know." Assuming they were finished, Emily was reaching for the diaper bag when the doctor added, "Earlier, while I was going through Mary Kate's file, I noticed that we don't have a medical history on your sperm donor. I can't understand how that slip-up occurred. Whenever a child is conceived through in vitro, a thorough medical history on the donor is required by law. It's standard procedure in this office to include the information in the child's records—just in case any genetically based complications arise in the future." Dr. Simpson fixed Emily with a hopeful look. "Do you happen to know who your donor was?"

Emily gaped at him, stunned. "What do you mean? Of course I do. Keith was the donor."

Dr. Simpson frowned. "Emily, you must be mistaken. Keith couldn't have been the donor. He was sterile. That's why in vitro, using an anonymous donor's sperm, was necessary."

Dillon jerked to a halt, his gaze fixing on Emily.

"What? That's ridiculous!" she exclaimed. "Keith wasn't sterile. The problem was with me, not my husband. He went over all my tests himself and told me that I had to have in vitro to conceive because my fallopian tubes were blocked with scar tissue."

"Mmm." Sitting at the small, built-in desk, the doctor tapped on the computer keyboard and studied the screen.

Watching him, Emily's chest grew painfully tight, as though a cold hand were squeezing her heart. This was all a hideous mistake, she told herself. It had to be.

"Not according to this. The test results in your file show that there's nothing wrong with you." He tapped some more, scrolling down. "Under Reason for Procedure it says, husband sterile."

"What? But...that can't be. Mary Kate is Keith's child. Not some stranger's."

"Doctor, could we talk about this some other time?" Dillon interjected.

"No." Emily shook her head. "No, I want to clear this up now. This is absurd. Someone has made a mistake. For heaven's sake, just look at Mary Kate." She gestured toward her daughter, who was still sniffling in Dillon's arms. "She looks just like...Kei..." Emily's eyes widened as her gaze settled on Dillon and her daughter, their faces just inches apart. "Oh, dear Lord."

The look in Dillon's eyes confirmed the truth she was trying so desperately to push away, and the hand around her heart squeezed tighter.

"There is no mistake," he said in a flat voice. "I'm Mary Kate's father. My brother asked me to donate sperm. He wanted the child to carry our family genes."

Emily made a distressed sound and sank down onto the room's only vacant chair. She was going to be sick.

Dr. Simpson looked back and forth between Dillon's grim face and Emily's shocked one. "I see. Well, that explains the resemblance." He cleared his throat. "Obviously you two need to go home and have a long talk and sort this out. So I'll leave you to it." He rose and left the room quietly, leaving behind a thick silence.

Emily and Dillon stared at each other. The air seemed to vibrate between them, filled with a palpable tension.

Suddenly she broke eye contact and shot to her feet, reaching for the diaper bag.

"Emily, he's right. We have to talk."

"No!" She shook her head vehemently, though she still did not look at him. "Not now. Not here." She stuffed Mary Kate's favorite rattle and bottle of juice back into the bag, hooked the strap over her shoulder and marched out the door, leaving him no choice but to follow.

They made the drive back to the apartment in silence. Emily sat with her arms crossed, pressed against the passenger door, and stared out the side window. She felt as though she was about to fly apart at any second. Out of the corner of her eye she noticed Dillon's frequent glances, but she could not bring herself to look at him, or speak.

He had lied to her. Betrayed her.

When he brought the car to a halt in the parking garage of their building she hopped out of the car and unstrapped Mary Kate from her car seat before Dillon had a chance to retrieve her. Clutching the infant to her breast, she headed for the elevators, leaving him to bring the diaper bag.

They rode up to the penthouse in silence, the tension between them so thick you could feel it. The baby had fallen asleep on the ride home, and when they entered the apartment Emily carried her straight to the nursery and put her to bed. Dillon followed and stowed the diaper bag in its customary place beside the changing table. After covering the baby she turned to find him watching her, but she ignored him and crossed the hall to their bedroom. He followed right on her heels.

"Emily, let me explain—"

"No!" she exploded, whirling to face him. Her whole world had just caved in on top of her, and he wanted to *talk!* All she wanted at that moment was to scream and scratch and kick and pummel until the awful pressure in her chest subsided. "I don't want to hear your excuses!" she shouted. "There is nothing you can say that will make this right! Besides, I've had enough of your lies!"

"I've never lied to you," he protested. Then he winced in response to her blistering glare. "All right, all right. Maybe I did by omission. That was wrong. I know that, but I swear to you, I was going to tell you everything."

"When? When Mary Kate graduated from college?"

"Tonight. I was going to tell you tonight after dinner."

"Oh please. What do you take me for, an idiot? You've had a year to tell me. Actually, telling me should never have become an issue. I should have been told that Keith was sterile. I know that many women are so desperate for a child of their own that they're willing to use an anonymous sperm donor, and I'm not judging them. If that's what they want, I have no problem with it. But the decision whether or not to have another man's baby is the mother's to make. In this case it was mine to make.'' She thumbed her chest angrily. ''*Mine!* Not Keith's. And certainly not yours!''

Dillon grimaced and held up his hands. ''You're right. You're absolutely right. And believe me, I tried to tell Keith that, but he would not listen.''

''But you went along with his plan anyway, didn't you?''

''Because I felt I had no choice. If I hadn't, Keith would have used an anonymous donor.''

The statement hit her like a slap in the face, and she reeled back under this new blow. Horrified, she stared at Dillon, and felt herself pale as the blood drained from her face.

''No,'' she protested feebly, shaking her head. ''No, I don't believe you. Not even Keith would have done something that underhanded.'' But even as the words left her lips she knew that he would have. Keith had always put his own needs and wants before anyone else's, without a thought—or a care—to the right or wrong of it.

''Maybe not. But I wasn't confident enough of that to risk it. I guess I figured you'd prefer to have my child rather than a complete stranger's.''

''I would have preferred to have a choice,'' she snapped. ''And don't you dare try to whitewash your part in all this. Maybe you thought you were doing me a favor. I don't know. But at the very least, after Keith was killed, you should have told me. Instead you lied to me and tricked me into believing you actually cared about me.''

''I *do* care about you. I love you, Emily.'' Dillon's

eyes entreated. He took a step toward her, his hand outstretched, but she retreated.

"*Stop it!*" she cried, panic nearly choking her. She didn't trust herself to let him touch her. She loved him too much. And she wanted so badly for him to make this awful pain go away. It would be so easy to put her head on his shoulder and pretend that he really did love her. She wanted so much for that to be true. But it wasn't, and she had to face that.

"Don't you dare say that to me. Not now. Not ever again. I don't know how you have the nerve. We both know that the only reason you married me was so you could gain custody of your daughter."

"Emily!" He looked as though she had slapped him. "Sweetheart, no. That's not true." He reached out to her again and again she retreated, but when she backed into the wall she panicked and slapped furiously at his hands.

"Stop it! Don't touch me!" She ducked under his arm and tore out of the room and across the hall.

"Emily, wait!" Dillon called, hurrying after her, but as he reached the nursery she slammed the door in his face. Dillon jiggled the doorknob, but it was locked fast. "Emily, please. We can't fix this if you won't talk to me."

"No! Just go away."

Frustrated, Dillon cursed under his breath. He didn't know what to do. He knew he could easily break the door down, but he didn't want to frighten her. Or Mary Kate. Nor did he want to carry on a conversation with a door between them. He gritted his teeth and looked down the hallway, debating. Maybe he should let her calm down. Right now she was so upset she was hysterical and not thinking straight. It was probably best to back off and give her some space, let her get her emotions under control. They could talk then.

A choking sound came from inside the nursery, then another, and another. Dillon frowned. What the—? Then the sound gave way to a long, eerie wail, and he realized that she was crying.

Grimacing, he closed his eyes and rested his forehead against the door. "Ah, sweetheart."

Dillon expected, or at least hoped, that Emily would calm by that evening and come to bed, but she spent the night in the nursery, on the daybed, he assumed. The next morning the door was still locked and there was no sound from inside. She was probably still worn out from that crying jag, he told himself. Deciding he would give her more time, he left her a note telling her that he loved her and he would be home early to talk, and went to work.

That evening, however, when he let himself into the apartment a disquieting silence greeted him. "Emily?" He stood in the middle of the living room and waited for an answer, but none came. The hair on the back of his neck began to prickle as he headed down the hallway. "Emily, where are you?"

There was no sign of her in the bedroom or the adjoining bath. Dillon stood in the middle of the room and looked around for a note, but there wasn't one. Then his gaze lit on the closet, and a feeling of dread settled over him. He crossed the room in three long strides and jerked open the door and his knees nearly gave way beneath him. Emily's side was empty.

He stared at the empty hangers, then spun away and charged across the hall. The diaper bag was missing. So was the baby quilt that always hung over the end of the crib. One after another, he jerked open the drawers of the baby bureau. Nothing.

They were gone.

Dillon spent the weekend sitting by the telephone waiting for Emily to call. By Monday he was half out of his mind and going stir-crazy. For four days he did not go to work, not to any of the various construction sites or his main offices. Nor did he call.

He spent the entire time driving around, searching for Emily's car, on the streets and in the parking lots of hotels and apartments all over that part of town. At one point he was so desperate he drove by Adele's town house, though he knew that was the last place she'd go—or be welcomed.

Houston was a city of millions. He knew it was like looking for the proverbial needle in a haystack, but he had to do something.

When he returned home each evening he raced to the answering machine, but there was never a message from Emily. Six days crawled by, and he barely ate or slept. The small hours of the night usually found him roaming the apartment, or standing beside the empty crib, feeling like someone had ripped his heart out.

By Friday he finally accepted that his efforts were futile and, short of hiring a private detective to hunt her down, which he wasn't yet ready to do, he was not going to find Emily, so he might as well go to work.

When he walked into the site office, except for a disapproving glance at the dark circles under his eyes, Gert barely looked up, nor did she question his unexplained absence. He was so worried and distracted several hours passed before the strangeness of that occurred to him.

Gert was as blunt as they came and because of the special bond between them she felt no compunction whatsoever about tearing strips out of his hide if she felt he deserved it. Normally she would've been snapping at him like a junkyard dog the instant he stepped foot in the door, demanding to know where he'd been. Come to that, she hadn't called his apartment even once these past four days.

Abandoning the blueprints spread out on his desk, Dillon went to the door and studied his assistant. Looking up from her work, she gave him a carefully neutral smile, which in itself was strange. Dillon's eyes narrowed. Something wasn't right here, he thought. She'd been entirely too docile all morning.

Like a bolt out of the blue, it occurred to him that Emily had lost contact with the people in her old set. Most were medical people, and more Keith's friends than hers, and after the funeral they had stopped calling her. The only friend Emily had made since Keith's death was Gert.

Of course. Why hadn't he thought of that before? Gert was genuinely fond of Emily. Though she was his trusted right hand and unofficial surrogate mother, it would be just like her to take in his wife and daughter and never say a word to him, if Emily asked her not to. He knew, also, if his suspicions were correct, confronting Gert would be a waste of time.

That evening, playing his hunch, Dillon drove to Gert's home. When she opened the door she gave him a disgusted look and snapped, ''Well, it's about time you figured it out,'' and stepped aside to let him in.

The instant he entered the living room his gaze zeroed in on Emily. She sat curled in one corner of the sofa, listlessly flipping through a magazine. At her feet, in her springy canvas seat, Mary Kate kicked her legs and waved her arms and bounced.

He drank in the sight of them, his throat so tight it hurt. "Hello, Emily."

Her head jerked up, and his heart contracted at the raw panic in her eyes. She grabbed the baby and bounded to her feet, and like a tigress protecting her young, she clutched the infant to her breasts. Mary Kate spotted him and began to kick excitedly.

"How did you find me?" Emily looked at Gert.

"Don't blame her. She didn't say a word. I played a hunch."

"I'll get out of your way and let you two talk," Gert murmured.

Emily looked panic-stricken. "No! Don't leave," she pleaded, but the older woman had already disappeared into the kitchen.

Emily glared at Dillon and clutched the baby tighter. "I won't let you take her," she declared angrily. "I don't care how much money you have or how many powerful people you know, I'll fight you. Mary Kate is *mine!*"

"Good Lord, Emily! Surely you don't believe I would try to take her from you?" That she could even think such a thing cut him to the quick. "I would never do that. Don't you know I'd rip my heart out rather than hurt you? Yes, I love Mary Kate. But I love you, too. I have since the moment we met," he declared quietly, throwing caution to the wind.

Emily's eyes widened, then narrowed warily. "I

don't believe you. You're just saying that so I'll come back and you can have Mary Kate."

"No, it's true. Why else do you think I agreed to be the sperm donor for your child?"

"You were doing a favor for Keith," she shot back.

"No. I did it for you. Because I love you."

Emily lifted her chin. "After all that's happened, how do you expect me to believe you? Even if I wanted to, I'd never really know for sure, would I?"

"Oh, for heaven's sake, I've listened to all of this nonsense I can take," Gert declared, stomping back into the room. That she had been shamelessly eavesdropping was evident, but she showed not an ounce of remorse.

"Dammit, Gert, stay out of this," Dillon barked. "This is between Emily and me."

"Oh, hush up, boy. I'm on your side." She turned to Emily and planted her hands on her hips. "Now, you listen to me, young lady. Dillon is telling the truth. I know because he's kept a snapshot of you in his desk for years. Not you and Keith. Just you. He used to take it out and stare at it when he thought no one was around."

"Dammit, Gert. That was private. What the hell were you doing, snooping in my desk?"

"Oh, calm down. How many times over the years have you asked me to find something you misplaced? Of course I went through your desk. I've done it a thousand times."

Dillon groaned, raking his hand through his hair.

Emily gazed at Dillon, shocked. "You have a photo of me?"

"Didn't I just say that?" Gert demanded indignantly. "If you don't believe me, you can look for yourself. It's at the back in the bottom left-hand drawer, hidden between the pages of an accounts journal."

"And you just happened to accidentally find it there?" Dillon drawled. "Right."

Gert ignored him. "I always figured the woman in that picture was the love of Dillon's life, but something had torn the two of you apart. It never occurred to me that you were Keith's wife. Then you walked into the office that first morning, and all the pieces to the puzzle fell into place.

"I've watched him moon over your picture for seven long years, so don't try to tell me he married you to get custody of his daughter. He loves her, sure, but it was you he wanted. He always has. That man loves you to distraction. Don't you ever doubt it.

"True, what he did was wrong. Although you have to admit, he was in a tough spot. He knew Keith wasn't bluffing. If Dillon hadn't gone along with him he would have found someone else. I think you know that, too.

"Now, mind you, no one disputes that the decision should have been yours, or that you have a right to be angry that you were deceived. But before you make a decision you may regret, think about this. If Dillon hadn't gone along with Keith, you wouldn't have Mary Kate."

Emily felt the blood drain from her face. Instinctively, she clutched the baby tighter. She hadn't thought of it that way.

Pleased by her reaction, Gert forged on. "Dillon made a doozie of a mistake that made a tangled mess of your lives, but his heart was in the right place. If you love him as you claim, you'll forgive him and move on. If you don't, you all lose."

Emily's heart boomed in her chest like a kettle drum. Did she dare believe that Dillon loved her? She desperately wanted to, but after the mistakes she'd made, she no longer trusted her instincts.

Still...Gert was the most brutally honest person she had ever known. She wouldn't lie, not even for Dillon. If she said he loved her, it must be true.

Her gaze switched to her husband. If she had the power to go back in time and control events, would she change anything? And risk never falling in love with Dillon, never marrying him? Never having Mary Kate?

Her heart answered instantly, emphatically. No. That was unthinkable.

Suddenly she felt as though an iron weight had lifted off her heart, and the constant aching pressure that she'd carried with her this past week melted away.

Maybe things really do happen for a reason, Emily thought. She had always heard that the road to true love was never smooth. She almost smiled. If that was true, then she and Dillon must be the world's greatest lovers. Lord knew, they'd certainly traveled a long, rocky, twisting path littered with potholes and pitfalls to find each other.

Happiness began to effervesce inside her like tiny champagne bubbles. Suddenly she felt lighter than air.

"I love you, Emily. I always will," Dillon vowed. He waited, watching her intently for some reaction. When he could stand her silence no longer he groaned. "For Pete's sake, have mercy. *Say* something. *Anything*."

Slowly, the corners of Emily's mouth curved upward. ''I love you, too, my darling.'' Smiling serenely, she hitched Mary Kate higher on her shoulder and walked into her husband's arms.

* * * * *

Don't miss Ginna Gray's
compelling new novel,

PALE MOON RISING.

This evocative, emotional tale of used-to-be lovers Olivia and Joe Connally is due out in Spring, 2003. Only from Mira Books!